Ruby Dixon

THE HALF-ORC'S MAIDEN BRIDE
Special Trade Paperback Edition

1theclub1@gmail.com

First Edition: April 2022
Special Trade Paperback Edition: October 2023
www.rubydixon.com

Cover and stepback artwork: Nisha Wilcox
Facebook: Neesh Wilcox
Instagram: @neesh_ipb_quarantine

Interior and cover design: Kati Wilde
Stock images licensed from Adobe Stock.

the HALF-ORC'S Maiden Bride

RUBY DIXON

YSHREM
Rockmourn Keep
Cragshold Keep
Godspine Mountains
Adassia
Blood Glacier
CHANDRILHAR
Tadekha's Citadel
Dirtlands
Aventine
BALSINGRA
Ghosthollow Murk
SUNSWALLOW
Sea of Storms
PORT TIDEWATER

Iolanthe

The day I grew taller than my father was the day I realized I'd be unwed forever. My mother's people are Yshremi, from a land of scholars and knowledge traders. She was delicate. Small. Pretty. My father's people are the sturdier Adassians, and unfortunately, I take after them. I am tall. Strong. My shoulders are broad and my hips broader. This wouldn't be a problem if my parents were rich.

They are *not* rich.

When I sprout up, I know my father's thoughts before he voices them. He can marry off a pretty daughter to further my family's fortunes, but a tall daughter with a plain face? I am useless to him. It doesn't matter that I dress myself in the prettiest gowns available, that I hunch my shoulders to hide my height, or bind my breasts and adjust my belts to make my thick, strong body seem more willowy. I cover myself in lotions day and night so that my skin might be soft and pretty, but as if the gods are determined to insult me, I am covered head to toe in freckles. I do not even have the fortune to be blonde. My hair, white-gold as a child, turns to a muddy brown the moment my breasts come in.

In short, I am strong and I have nice skin. I will make a fantastic spinster aunt to my siblings' children. I cannot even aspire to be a cleric of the gods, as temples must be bribed, and we have no money for the bribing.

(That suits me well enough. While clerists are great readers—which I enjoy—they are also great healers, and I find I do not have the stomach for such things.)

I try not to worry about my lack of appeal to a husband. After all, I have five younger sisters and my mother to spend time with, and I can avoid my father's baleful gaze if I'm careful. But then my mother dies from a wasting sickness. And then, one by one, my sisters—all pretty, delicate things that take after my mother's Yshremi blood—marry off. They marry farmers and merchants, and one marries a titled knight despite the fact that we are penniless.

Eventually, it is just me at home with Father. My siblings are gone, my mother in her final rest, and my father's remote hold in the rocky crag-lands of Adassia, Rockmourn Keep, grows poorer by the day. The woales, our beasts of burden, are sold off to pay retainers, then the pigs. My mother's jewelry disappears and when the fine, old tapestries disappear off the walls and my books vanish, I start to wonder what will be left for my father to sell.

I know it will not be me. He cannot even give me away. Perhaps he will cut my hair and make me ride with his men as a knight and pretend I am a man. Or perhaps I should run away and seek my own fortune. One night, I study my face, trying to decide if I will pass as a boy, but my breasts are too big, my mouth too full and pink to be anything but a woman's. So much for that.

I am stuck at Rockmourn Keep with my father until it crumbles to stones around us.

But since I have nowhere else to go, I hide my books, I keep smiling, and I make the best of things.

On my thirtieth birthday, Cook bakes me a tiny cake and I read letters from my sisters in the sunshine of the gardens, determined to enjoy my day. Two of them are pregnant, and the youngest just had her second child. They do not ask when I will marry. No one ever does. I try not to be envious. I've been tall for a very, very long time, so it's not as if my fate is surprising to me. I'm just...wistful. I don't know if I want to be a mother, but I'd like a home of my own...a husband of my own.

Something—anything—to call my own.

When my father arrives home that night, however, he has no gift for me. Instead, he smirks at me from across the dinner table. "Pack your things," he tells me. "I've found you a husband. We leave for his keep tomorrow."

"A husband?" I ask, scarcely daring to hope. I set my knife down next to my bowl, afraid my hands will tremble and I'll make a mess at the table. I don't want to give my father anything to criticize. "A husband would be...everything I dreamed of."

He grunts, cutting his food. "Good. I won't have you causing me trouble on this."

Causing him trouble? He knows I long for a husband, to be married. He knows of the romantic novels I pestered all the merchants to bring me, back when we had coins to spend. I try to contain my excitement, but it's difficult. I eat my food with careful bites, trying to think of questions that won't offend my father, because I desperately need him to tell me more about my husband-to-be. "Who is it?" I ask carefully. "A neighbor?"

The keep's great hall is silent as I wait for my father to respond, but the only sound is the scrape of his utensils against his plate. "His land is two days' ride from here."

So close, but not too close. I mentally go through all of the local lords I've met over the years, who has a son about my age, or a knight that is unattached. I can picture no one. "Who—"

"Never you mind," he says. "He is a strong warrior looking for a bride and he's willing to pay for you. That's all that's important."

He's giving my father a dowry for me? My eyes go wide. That's…unheard of. Most of the time, a bride must be sent with gold to her husband's family. It's one reason why I've remained unmarried for so long. Our keep is strong, our lands vast, but we are poor as paupers. Who in all the gods would pay my father for his tall, plain spinster daughter? Perhaps one of the border lords looking to broker a trade agreement? "Is he…Yshremi?"

That seems to amuse my grim father. "No. I can assure you, he's not. We go south to meet him, not north."

I didn't think so. Despite the fact that my mother was Yshremi, my father holds no love for their people. I lick my dry lips, my thoughts scattered. "Is he…tall?"

"If I tell you he is short and squat, it will not change the fact that you are to marry him," my father says irritably. "Aye, he is tall, and I will not have you hounding me. Know that we leave at first light, so pack your things, and do not give me trouble on this, Iolanthe. I need his coin to protect these lands, and I need the swords he will trade me for your hand in marriage. If you ruin this, you doom us all. Understand?"

My stomach knots with worry. Since it is the Anticipation, tensions between Yshrem and Adassia have been high. There have been raids all along the borders, and I know my father worries he will not be able to pay his knights to keep his lands secure. I think of the farmers with their small children, the sheepherders who depend on my father for protection from roving bands of outlaws, or worse, the wild Cyclopae who rule the kingdom of Yshrem. Rumor has it they have turned their eyes southward, toward Adassia.

I decide I do not care if my husband is short (though a tall woman like me would vastly prefer a husband of her size). As long as he is kind, that is all that matters.

Please, I pray to the gods and goddesses. Let him be kind.

I **cannot sleep that night. I think of my upcoming marriage,** and I am giddy with excitement. Will my husband kiss me on the lips? I daydream of my husband demanding sweet kisses from me, and then I am so overwrought that I cannot think straight. I compose letters to all my sisters, telling them of my marriage and that I will write them after I am settled. Then, I take up needle and thread and sew dainty ruffles onto my best gown, so I can go to my new husband looking somewhat pretty and stylish instead of like a pauper's daughter. I enjoy sewing, and I'm good at it. I've become an expert at modifying old dresses to make them look new by adding colorful inserts or changing the seams of a bodice. I do so this night, lowering the neckline of my wedding gown so that my new husband might see my cleavage and swoon with delight at the sight of my bust.

Oh, I do hope he's tall.

When dawn arrives, I am twitching with readiness. My hair is braided tightly against my scalp and I wear my plainest dress for the ride. My pack is small, my modified wedding dress inside it, along with a few of the books I've secreted away, and a few spare chemises. I don't have much to bring to the marriage, but it sounds like my husband will not mind. I kiss Cook and hug the other servants, who have been my friends all these years, and then meet my father out by the stables. The remaining woales are saddled, their fat flanks weighted on each side with packs. To my surprise, my father's knights are all armed and wearing their leathers, their expressions grim as their horses prance in readiness.

Knights? Perhaps this is a show of strength to my new bridegroom. Then, I realize that of course my father must bring his knights—they are returning home with my bride-price. Smiling at my foolishness, I tie my pack to the woale and sit in one of the side-saddles, my father balancing out the other side. Woales are good for long distance travels and carrying packs, but they don't keep up well with horses, so it surprises me to see that both will be in our party.

But I don't ask. My father looks moody this morning, his

expression sour. He seems on edge, and I don't want to give him any reason to turn around and cancel my marriage. I just smile and look excitedly at the horizon.

In a few days, I shall finally be married. I will be a spinster no longer.

My first inkling that something is amiss comes when we ride south, and farther south still. Most of the largest settlements are along the river, which winds its way through the northern parts of Adassia. Father has always complained that the southern lands are full of vagrants, monsters, and thieves. But perhaps my new husband is a lord with a remote keep? It would explain why he must send away for a wife, if there are few suitable noblewomen nearby. So I keep smiling, my head full of dreamy thoughts. In my mind, my new husband is tall—so very tall—and dark-haired. His features will be strong and rugged, his arms brawny, and he will have a deep, rumbly voice. And, I decide, he will insist upon kissing me the moment he sees me, so taken with my appearance. I sigh with delight at the thought.

I start to worry when Father sells the woale at a seedy-looking outpost on the second day, and the knights all dismount. I clutch my pack, doing my best not to ask questions. Father has a plan, I tell myself. He's worked this out with my new husband. I'm merely being a silly female.

Even so, it strikes me as odd that we're going to walk the rest of the way. "Are we a fair distance yet, Father?" I ask carefully. "The sun will be setting soon."

"Not far," Father says, his voice that curt tone that brooks no argument. "Keep up with the men."

I bite my lip and do as he says. It's really no difficulty to keep pace with the knights leading their horses. They're wearing armor (still) and my legs are long and strong. Even so, the fact that my husband's home is near this filthy little outpost is more than a little concerning.

I'm pretty sure I saw an orc in one of the shanty-like buildings, of all scandalous things. A green-skinned, shaven-headed orc. Horrifying. But I keep my gaze on the road ahead, because my future is ahead of me, not behind. I can always tell my new husband about the orc so he can take care of the situation.

As I walk beside the knights, I send another prayer up to Belara, the goddess of marriage. I pray that he will be kind, and generous, and loving. And then, because I cannot help myself, I pray for him to be tall. For him to be strong, with a deep voice and a broad chest, and that he is able to carry me. A girl can wish, after all. And even though I am no longer a girl, and taller than half of the knights, I enjoy my foolish dreams.

I am sure my husband will be…sufficient.

Toward dusk, a single, lonely outpost rises from the cliffs. The orange and purple skies illuminate the rolling hills of the landscape around us, and the cliffs ahead. As we approach, I see that the lone tower at the top of the cliffs is accompanied by what looks like a fortress built into the cliff itself. A stone wall surrounds the grounds themselves, a tidy courtyard for a natural fortress. Something niggles in the back of my mind, a rumor from last year. There was a stronghold to the south that was overrun, and I remember my father's worry that the bandits who took over would reach to the north and terrorize his lands.

Cragshold Keep. That was the name. I vaguely remember that it was held by fat old Lord Dramus, but I do not recall Dramus having any sons my age, just a boy no more than nine.

Oh gods, am I being sent to marry a child? *Belara, please, please*, I inwardly beg. *Please give me a good, strong, tall husband my age.* If I marry a child, I will not be his wife. I will end up being his mother…and I will never have children of my own. The age gap between us will be too great.

"Am I marrying someone from Lord Dramus's family?" I ask in a quivering voice.

"Hush yourself, girl," my father growls. "And do not bring up that name."

"But this is Cragshold Keep, is it not?" I remember the stories of its distinctive layout.

"It was," my father says, voice curt. "It has a new lord now. You'll be marrying him."

Oh. Relieved that I'm not to be marrying a child, I let out the breath I've been holding and relax. I think I can handle anything save for marrying a child.

Furtively, I smooth my wind-blown hair and skirts as we approach the front of the keep. I want to curse Father for making me walk, because now I'm disheveled and slightly sweaty, but I say nothing. Father is…well, Father. I learned long ago that unless I wanted a smack to the jaw and a comment about my height that would hurt worse than the strike, I'd say nothing at all.

So I remain quiet when we approach, and the roughest-looking group of men I've ever seen comes out to meet us. Due to the setting sun's glare, it takes me a moment to realize that they're not all men. Some of them are orc, which is alarming, and another with pointed ears and tanned skin and large, fanged teeth. I…I don't know what to make of this. They look like outlaws, their armor and clothes shoddy and rusty in some parts, the chainmail showing broken links in some parts. They're covered in weapons and they look dangerous and hard.

"Your lord is expecting us," is all my father says.

The men stare at me, gazing up at my height. One man elbows an orc, grinning, and my cheeks burn with shame. I hope the lord of this place doesn't find me as wanting as his men do. I don't understand why he's hiring brigands. It doesn't seem safe…but perhaps his need of coin is even greater than I thought.

That must be it, I realize. He needs coin so he hires ruffians. It takes me a moment to remember that he's paying my father for me and not the other way around, and my stomach twists in a terrified knot. Did…did no one tell him Lord Purnav's unmarried daughter is tall and broad? Surely word would have gotten around.

Surely Father would have told him.

I look over at my father, but he won't meet my eyes, and my stomach sinks even further. This feels like a trap. Is he deceiving the man I am to marry? I glance around as we stride into the courtyard of Cragshold Keep, and I don't see any other women, just more brigands that tend to horses and watch our party with a great deal of interest. My heart flutters in my chest like a trapped bird, and then like a frantic falcon when we abandon the mounts with one of the knights outside, and the rest of the retinue moves behind my father as we step inside the keep itself.

The interior is just as crowded, the overhead candelabrum

filled with melting candles that offer a warm orange glow to the great room. There's a massive stone fireplace and a long wooden table covered in dirty dishes and half-empty beer mugs. Men are everywhere, and so are hunting hounds. It looks like a keep that hasn't seen a woman's touch in…ever. I have to admit, the sight of all that filth gives me a secret thrill. It's not that I love dirt, but this is obviously a place that needs me.

My soon-to-be husband clearly needs a wife, and I'm confident I can get things running smoothly. I'm excellent at sewing and running a household, since I've run my father's ever since my mother passed. My youngest sister, Flora, always teased me for loving all the traditional feminine duties, but I do. I love pretty dresses and doing my hair and sewing and all the things important for a wife. Flora wanted to be a soldier and explore the vast forests to the east.

Me, I just wanted to be valued.

Ironic that Flora was the first of my sisters to marry and is now raising a daughter while I've been left a spinster.

No longer, I think, and the fluttering in my chest starts again. But I need to be certain that this man knows of my… faults. I can run a vast household and sew an intricate sleeve, but I cannot change my height. As everyone stares at me, I move closer to my father. "Father? A word?"

Father turns, and his expression is ferociously angry. "Do not ruin this for me, Iolanthe—"

Ruin this? "But—"

His face is nearly purple with rage, his muttonchops trembling as spittle forms in the corners of his mouth. "You are marrying this lord, and that is final. You are not going to ruin this for me with your idle daydreams. He is a strong, fearsome lord. You should be grateful anyone will accept you at all."

I flinch, casting my gaze down in shame. Tears threaten, but I don't want my new husband's first sight of me to be a bright red nose, blotchy cheeks, and puffy eyes, so I do my best to fight away the urge to weep.

"Do not ruin this for me," Father hisses, leaning over me. "We need these funds desperately. If we do not get them, our knights will leave because they are not being paid. If they leave, we will be overrun by thieves and squatters within a month. Do you hear what I am saying, Iolanthe? You *have* to marry this man. The fate of everyone at home depends on you."

"I understand, Father," I whisper, sniffing. A tear escapes despite my best efforts.

"Quit sniveling," he snarls at me. "You're sore enough on the eyes as it is, and he needs to think he's getting a good deal with you. If I had any other daughters left to give away, I would, but all I've got left is you—"

"If you're done flattering my bride, I'd like to take a look at her," says a rich, smooth voice from behind us.

Oh, by all the gods. That must be my new husband, and he's heard Father upbraiding me. The shame of it burns, but I quickly swipe at my tears and straighten my dress, then compose myself, lifting my head. I turn, my hands clasped at my waist—

—and cannot help the gasp of horror that escapes me.

Standing behind us, wearing the same piecemeal, shoddy armor as the rest of the unruly soldiers, is an orc. He wears a lord's circlet atop his brow, and his black hair is pulled into a long tail at the base of his head. His skin is the dusky green of dried herbs and he's got one foot up on one of the benches as he leans forward, massive, hairy forearms resting atop his knee.

He smiles at us, revealing a pair of tusks—one of which is broken.

An orc. An orc *lord*. My father has sent me here to marry an orc.

I feel faint.

Agakor

My bride is here.

From the moment I clap eyes on the woman, I know she's mine. She strides up to my keep with big, shiny eyes, her dark hair pulled into a fancy braid woven atop her head like a crown. Even though she wears a pack on her shoulders, she keeps pace with the soldiers and from a distance, I can tell that she's taller than most of them.

This pleases me, as does the sight of her up close. I wasn't sure what to expect when Lord Purnav of Rockmourn offered his last unmarried daughter in exchange for a hefty bride-price and for a peace truce between us. The money is nothing. The peace truce is easily broken, but I admit the idea of a human bride—a willing human bride—appealed to me. A bride that comes from good family would give my claim on Cragshold Keep legitimacy and would downplay my half-orc heritage and the fact that a great many of my men are orcs. Even though I purchased the keep fairly from the old lord, we're treated like squatters and brigands by the neighboring lords.

I mean for that to end, and to establish my family's hold here. I want my sons to inherit this place, and for that, I need a bride.

I watch the female with narrowed eyes, gauging her reaction.

She's frightened. Any fool could see that. She's trembling head to toe, and it's clear from her wide, dark eyes that she had no idea she was to marry a half-orc. She doesn't scream or cry or even look at her father, which is a good sign. She simply smooths her dress with nervous hands and bites on her lip, perhaps to keep from screaming.

I rub my jaw. I'm not the most attractive of men. Orc genes are strong and I look far more like my father than my Cyclopae mother. I have the large features and black, heavy brows of my father's people, and my skin is almost as green as his was. My tusks are smaller and I am slightly less in height, but to a human, I am still a towering wall of muscle, broader and thicker than even the strongest of knights. She is likely not very pleased.

But that can be fixed. "I am pleased you've brought my bride, Lord Purnav. Step forward, woman. I would look properly at you." I can already see her, but I want to see her reaction to my words. To see how she reacts now that there is no getting away from the fact that she is here to marry the half-orc lord of this disorderly keep. I want to see how many tears I'll have to deal with, and if she'll squeal in horror when I touch her. Lord Purnav promised a willing, tall, comely daughter.

She's tall and comely enough, but it's clear she's not very willing.

The chit swallows hard, her throat visibly bobbing, and takes a brave step forward, her eyes averted as if she's afraid to look at me. Up close, I can see that her skin is lovely, soft and inviting and begging to be touched, and her lashes long and thick. She is covered in freckles on every bit of exposed skin, and I wonder if she's freckled everywhere. I can't wait to find out.

The woman clears her throat. "M-might I have a word with you, Lord…"

"Agakor," I supply. "Agakor of Broketusk Clan."

"Lord Broketusk," she stammers, still not meeting my gaze. Her hands are clasped tight in front of her at her waist, in a very ladylike fashion, but I can see just how white her knuckles are. "Might I have a word in private—"

Her words are drowned out by the hooting of my men. "She wants him in private already! Agakor's gonna have himself a son before the year is out, mark my words!"

More ribald shouts accompany this.

The woman's face drains of color, and her father looks impatient. He grabs the woman by the arm, hissing something in her ear. She hunches her shoulders a little, trying to seem smaller, and I decide I don't like the hand he puts on her.

I turn and glare at my men. "*Lady* Iolanthe may of course have a word in private with me. And the next person that shouts something obscene in front of my bride-to-be will have his tongue pulled out with the blacksmith's pliers."

The men just laugh, knowing I won't do any such thing, but the poor chit looks utterly faint. Her father gives her one last hissing, whispered command and then shoves her forward, and it takes everything I have not to grab him by the throat and toss him bodily out of my keep. It's a good thing I don't intend to keep my end of the bargain, because the urge to kill this fool is rising by the moment.

I offer the woman my arm to escort her, and she gives me a startled look, her gaze finally flashing to mine. By all the gods, those dark eyes are beautiful. Thickly lashed and deep in color, and so expressive. I decide then and there that Lady Iolanthe is going to be mine, no matter how the marriage negotiations go. No doubt she is asking me to meet with her in private so she can prettily tell me that her father did not explain that she would be marrying an orc, and there must be some mistake, and how she needs to return home with him.

And then I will simply tell her no.

Lady Iolanthe is not leaving this keep again unless it's as my wife.

She swallows audibly and then places her hand on my arm, gazing at the floor again as I lead her through the crowd. My men grin, pleased that we've finally got an honorable lady in the keep to be my bride. They know how important it is to me and to our band to be taken seriously. I escort her through the main hall, over to my private war room, where I keep my weapons and shields. There are pieces of armor everywhere, I notice, as we enter the room, and for every book on my shelves, there is also a vambrace or a melted candle, or even an old crust of bread. I try to envision this from her eyes and wonder if it will make her run in terror. Perhaps I should have ordered the men to take a day off of training and clean up first. I don't want her disappointed.

Well, more disappointed than she already is.

Once I lead her into my study, I shut the heavy wooden door behind me. "Speak your words. No one will hear them now save me."

And I wait. Wait for the excuses. The "there must be some mistake" speech.

She trembles again, such a soft, shy thing, and then wrings her hands. "I-I would know exactly what my father promised you," she says in a whisper-soft voice, tinier than the one she used in the hall. "I just..." Again, she wrings her hands. "I fear my father has oversold things."

"Has he, now," I say flatly. Here it comes.

Lady Iolanthe chews on her lip, reddening it. She has nice teeth, at least. "I fear..." She wrings her hands again. "There is much that rides upon our marriage. The funds..." She trails off, frowning to herself. "My father," she tries again. "He would very much like for this marriage to go through."

She won't look me in the eye, which I find I'm growing impatient with. "Spit it out, woman."

"O-oh, of course," she says, twisting her hands again in that helpless sort of way. "It's just...I know this is not what you expected." She bites her lip again. "I am very tall and not young, and I fear my father has oversold my virtues. I w-wished to apologize for that in private if he has misled you."

I don't think I have ever been so startled in my life.

She's apologizing to *me?* For being tall? And older? As if those things are a problem? I decide to take matters into my hands. I move to her side and put my finger under her chin, forcing her to look up at me. She tries to drop her gaze even as she lifts her chin, shy thing that she is. "Look at me," I growl, and she trembles again. "Look at me, Iolanthe."

Those dark, liquid eyes meet mine and I can tell she's startled by my nearness. Then, her gaze travels up and up, to the top of my head. Her lips part. "You…you're very tall," she breathes.

"I am." I run my thumb along the delicate line of her jaw. "I heard your father had a tall, unmarried daughter that ran his keep. It was I that approached him and asked for marriage. I knew you were a strapping woman, and this was a benefit to me. I do not wish to try and kiss some tiny bit of a thing that only comes to my waist."

Those lashes flutter up at me, and her lips part, as if she's surprised. "You…want me to be tall?"

"Aye, it suits me quite well. As for your age, I am five and thirty myself. Were you any younger than you are, I might feel as if I'm robbing a cradle."

She licks her lips, her pink tongue darting out. "I see. Then…I do not need to apologize?" Those gorgeous eyes meet mine again. "Or beg you to marry me?"

"Oh, sweet lady, you can beg me all you like," I purr. "But we are marrying regardless."

"I see," she breathes. "Well, all right, then."

"And you?" I prompt. "Your father did not tell you who I was, did he?"

"He did not tell me you were an orc, no."

"Half-orc. My mother was a Cyclopae warrior."

Her gaze flies to mine, surprised. "You have Cyclopae blood?" At my nod, she actually looks pleased. "That is…pleasant. Nice. My mother was Yshremi and the queen there recently married a Cyclopae king. My father…" She trails off and then wears a little bright smile. "My father is a brave, strong man, but he is Adassian."

Clever chit will not say anything ill about him. Interesting.

Her lips part and she looks at me and then snaps her mouth shut again.

"Say it," I demand, half expecting her to demur. My mother was a fierce woman who took no shit from anyone. She would just as soon punch my father as she would kiss him. This tender little morsel is of my mother's height, but nothing like her in personality. "Speak what you are thinking."

Her face goes pale, her cheeks two spots of crimson, and she drops her gaze again. "I…merely thought of…the upcoming marriage…"

And when her face turns even redder, I realize what she is refusing to say. She thinks of Cyclopae marriages. Of the three days of ceremony.

Of the revealing of the bride. The tasting of the bride, and the bedding of the bride.

I was not going to insist upon it, but by the gods, I am now.

Iolanthe

Shock is making my senses slow, I suspect. Shock, and bitter irony.

Did I not pray to Belara to give me a tall husband? A strong husband with a deep voice and for him not to be younger than me? It seems I should have been more specific in my prayers. I should have also asked that he not be an orc.

An orc.

Rather, a half-orc, if what he says is true. And Father did not say one word of this to me. Orcs are raiders, ruffians who obey no laws. They live wild in the mountains like animals, if the Adassian stories are to be believed…and I am to marry one? I feel faint. I've always been a dutiful daughter, but I wonder this time if Father has pushed too far. I think of his words—how he said his keep will surely fall if he does not get my bride-price to fill his coffers again and to pay his knights. I think of the hard-working servants at the keep, the knights who patrol tirelessly, and the stablehands who have always been so very kind to me. I cannot let them lose their home.

It seems I am marrying an orc.

Blinking back tears, I keep my gaze lowered so he does not see my dismay. I cannot give him reason to call off the wedding. Bad enough that I have shown up windblown and not looking my best. I touch my nose, wondering if it is red from the wind. I hunch my shoulders, trying to hide my height just a little more, and I wring my hands. "Are you sure my height won't be an issue, my lord? I want you to be pleased."

"I would be pleased," he says in a low voice, "if you looked at me again."

I glance up, my cheeks hot with a blush. I've been around knights and men my entire life, but I've always been invisible. The spinster daughter, the one that runs the keep. The one that is tall and unappealing to look at. My sisters are all dainty things with pretty faces and sunny personalities, but I'm the shy one. It's hard to look him in the eye, knowing that we are to be married.

"Surely you must want to gaze upon an orc? Even for just a little?" His hard, wide mouth curves up on one side in a half-smile. "You have to be curious, unless your father told you all about me already."

I bite my lip. "He-he did not, my lord."

"Well." The orc—half-orc, I hastily correct myself—grins

wider. "For one, I do have a name and I'm not a lord."

Oh, gods. He told me his name and I've already forgotten it in my panic. I fight back a whimper. "M-might you tell me again?"

"Agakor," he murmurs, his voice surprisingly gentle. "Of Clan Broketusk. No lord about it."

"What should I call you?"

"Agakor will do…or husband." He tilts his head, regarding me. "Are you upset that I'm an orc?"

Oh gods! Such a difficult question. I try to think of the right way to answer it. "I w-was surprised, I admit. But I still need to marry you."

"Need?" One of those heavy, thick brows goes up. "Is your father forcing you?"

I shake my head violently. "N-no, of course not," I lie. In truth, Father has made it quite clear how he will feel if this marriage doesn't go through, but I'm not thinking of him. I'm thinking of everyone else that will be affected should we not get the funds to save my father's keep. "Please, my lord—I mean, Agakor. My father needs this alliance desperately."

"I know." His expression grows hard. "And he sends a terrified daughter to work diplomacy. He should be ashamed."

I bite my lip. Does he think I'm terrified because he's an orc? Does he think I am appalled because of his nature? Now that I've gotten past my initial shock and spoken to him, he seems kind enough. Like he has a sense of humor that Father does not. I can make do. "If it pleases you, know that I would be terrified even if you were the most handsome human lord in the land," I admit shyly. "Probably even more terrified then."

He chuckles. "Terrified of beauty? Why is that?"

"Because that handsome lord would not want me," I say softly. "He could have anyone." I glance up at Agakor (such an orkish name) and try not to flinch as I point out, "You could have anyone. With the bride-price you are paying, you could get a younger, prettier wife—"

"I know." His gaze glitters. "But I need a lady. And like I said before, your height pleases me. So look your fill and decide if you will go through with this marriage or not, because once we leave this room, the marriage ceremonies shall begin."

I want to laugh hysterically. As if I can look at him and decide that no, I do not wish to marry him. As if there are such options open to me, a lesser noblewoman of plain face, no fortune, and far too much height. I have nothing to draw a husband, and my father has made it quite clear that if I back out of this, everyone that lives at the keep will suffer. They will be out of work, and without knights to defend my father's keep against border raiders, how long before he loses everything? At least here, I can help my people.

At least here, I am guaranteed a roof and a bed, even if I must share it with an orc.

So even though I am terrified, I clasp my hands at my waist and try to look composed. "I have not changed my mind."

"Are you certain? I do not want you screaming or weeping with terror as we marry. It won't help my reputation. I'm already feared enough as it is. I need a wife to help me improve my reputation, not destroy it entirely."

I glance up at him and I could swear he's got a hint of a wry smile on his face and…a dimple? In one greenish cheek. Oh. For some reason, that dimple decides me. No one can be truly evil and have a dimple, can they? "I promise if I weep and cry, it will be in private."

He grimaces. "Can you try to look less terrified?"

I swallow hard and drop my eyes again, only for him to touch a finger to my chin and force me to meet his gaze once more. I manage a smile, and Agakor barks a laugh at how tremulous it is. I lift my head higher, trying to look defiant. I can't believe I'm trying to convince an orc that I'm going to be a good bride for him. Oh, Belara, of all the prayers I've sent to you, why answer this one and in this manner? "I'm ready to marry."

Part of me expects him to grunt, to drag me out of this room, and then for us to get the marriage over with. Instead, he gives me a thoughtful look. "If I'm to be seen as less orkish, I must marry you in the ways of my mother's people. You've heard of Cyclopae traditions?"

Only in the most lewd of stories. I remember giggling with my sisters about the spinster queen of Yshrem, and how she'd been forced to marry a Cyclopae warlord. How he'd insisted on parading her bared body before his court, and then he'd had her atop a table in front of all. It's utterly scandalous and absolutely without a lick of truth. "I have not," I decide, since tact feels like the best idea. "Could you educate me?"

He grimaces, which makes his big, broad face all the uglier and more orc-like, and something inside me quails. I could swear he looks like he's about to start sweating. "The Cyclopae have a three-day marriage ceremony, in which the bride and groom prove to each other that they are satisfied with their mate. The first step is the revealing of the bride, in which the bride is stripped bare in front of her husband-to-be's clan so she can show the beauty she brings to their marriage."

Oh.

Oh my goodness. All the torrid rumors about the Yshremi queen's marriage are true? "But…why?"

"It is a moment of pride for the woman. She shows her husband what she blesses his bed with."

I think of my too-long legs and strong thighs, and I'm not sure most men would consider that a blessing. I feel faint. This wedding that I wished for so much is becoming a nightmare. "And I am…to do this?"

"On the first day, yes."

Oh gods. First day. "And the second day?"

"The…ah, tasting of the bride."

I gasp in horror, my fingers digging into the belted waist of my dress. "You're going to eat me?"

Agakor stares at me like I've lost my mind. "Exactly how innocent are you, Iolanthe?"

I don't understand what he's getting at. "I am a maiden. Is that what you're asking? You have to eat maiden flesh?" My mouth is dry and I press a trembling hand to my lips. Perhaps… perhaps I can tell him that I'm not. Perhaps—

Agakor clears his throat. "Ah…it is a tasting of the bride. No more than tongue is used, this I promise. And again, it is supervised to make sure that the groom is capable of pleasuring his bride." He stares at me. "With his tongue."

I blink. A budding glimmer of realization makes me blush. Surely he doesn't mean…in a woman's secret places? "You mean like kissing?"

"I mean my tongue on your cunt, Iolanthe."

I gasp, my fingers digging into my dress again. No one has ever spoken so boldly to me. My pulse races, and I swallow hard. "Do...do Adassians do that?" I whisper, scandalized. "Do orcs? Or is it just Cyclopae..."

Agakor chuckles, rubbing the back of his neck. "Well, my love, I'd like to think that all men do it to their wives, but I know some don't. Rest assured, though, I'm an expert on such matters. I'd make sure you're thoroughly pleased."

"Oh." I snag my fingers into my belt, because I desperately need to hold on to something or I'm going to fall apart. My face feels like it's on fire. "Do you...would you want me to do the same? To you? My mouth? Er, licking?"

He groans, his eyes fluttering closed, and I'm surprised to see how thick and dark his lashes are. They're startlingly beautiful in that coarse face. "Only if you wanted to. I wouldn't demand it...but I would like it."

I bite my lip. "I've never seen a man naked." I've seen farm animals, though, and the bulls aren't built the same as the cows. "I wouldn't know what to expect."

Agakor tilts his head, studying me. "Would you like to see me naked? Before the wedding?"

My gaze flies to his face. "W-what?"

He puts up a hand. "I'm not saying that to be a lecher. This is all new for you, and I know that can be overwhelming. I'm committed to this marriage. If you are, I see no harm in showing you my body. But if you feel the slightest need to back out, then it's best if we don't, because if your father sends a war party out for my blood, I'd hate to have to murder them all."

I frown at that. He acts like it's a done deal, him winning. I want to ask about it, but...I have to admit, I'm far more curious to see him naked. Is that wrong? It feels wrong, and yet...he's offering and I'm so, so curious. I hesitate. "You...you'd show me what you look like? Without clothes?"

"Of course. You're to be my wife, are you not? I figure my body will belong to you just as much as yours will belong to me."

But...without clothes on? I purse my lips, because I'd never considered that a husband would see me naked. Of course he would. It's foolish of me to assume otherwise. I assume he would have to see under my skirts at any point for...reasons. I'm not sure what those reasons are just yet, but perhaps to put a baby there. Thoughts of babies make me pause. "If I see you naked, is it going to make me pregnant?"

Agakor's big hand goes to his brow. "Ah, lady. They've done you dirty, keeping you so innocent. No, I can't make you pregnant just with you looking. I assure you of that. I'd have to put my cock inside you to make you pregnant."

I want to ask where inside me, but of course I know that answer. And of course he can't make me pregnant simply by looking at me. That's not how the horses in the stable are bred either. My face flames. "I know that. I-I'm just flustered."

He grunts, his hand going to his belt. His dark eyes rest on me. "Did you want to see? Or is it too much for you? There is no pressure either way. I'm simply offering to ease your curiosity."

Do I want to see? I really do, if nothing else to answer questions I've had in the past. He has to put his cock inside me—as he says—to get me pregnant, so I'm curious what it will look like. I try to picture horse cocks, but I don't think I've paid that much attention to the underside of my father's horses, just that they mount the females and then I get hurried inside by someone because I need to protect my "maiden eyes." And now this orc—half-orc, I correct myself—is offering to undress just to satisfy my curiosity.

It feels like a trap. "Are you…trying to get out of marrying me?"

"Absolutely not." Agakor looks quite serious.

"Is this an attempt to see what's under my skirts before we marry?" He shakes his head, and his face looks trustworthy, oddly enough. One last question, then. "Are you going to tell my father if I say yes?"

"Lady, if there is anything that passes between us, it shall remain between us," he promises.

I bite my lip. "Then…I wish to see. And please call me Iolanthe if we are to marry."

My face feels like it's on fire, and part of me still waits for him to mock me, or tease that I want to take a look at his cock like some sort of shameless wanton. Orc cock, no less. My sisters would be appalled at my request, but…my choices are either spinsterhood and under Father's thumb forever, or marriage to this man. And when he smiles at me, that dimple showing in his odd green cheek, I feel flustered, but it's a good sort of flustered, not a bad one.

He doesn't mock me. In fact, he takes his belt, undoes it, and drops his pants, making good on his word.

Agakor

I thought that when I approached Lord Purnav about marrying his spinster daughter that she'd be someone I'd have to endure. Even a half-orc has standards, after all. I thought she'd be like him, unpleasant to look at and even less pleasant to speak to. I thought a lord's gently bred daughter would sneer at me and be someone I'd have to put up with to get an indisputable claim to my land, and later, an heir.

But Iolanthe is a revelation. Her beautiful, dark eyes watch me undress with eagerness. Her soft skin begs to be touched, and she looks…excited. She is beyond innocent if our conversation is to be believed, but there's no fear in her eyes, and this is the same female that begged me earlier to marry her, and that worried her father had oversold *her* value as a bride. To say that I am pleased with her is an understatement.

And when I reveal my cock to her, the startled gasp she makes is gratifying.

One hand flies to her wide-open mouth and her gaze flicks up to mine. "It's so…big!"

A gratifying thing to hear from one's bride-to-be. I ease my length out of my pants to make sure she can see the full package, the thick, veined shaft, tapered head, and my heavy sac. It's a deeper shade than the rest of my muted green skin, but I like to think it's a pleasant cock. The tavern wenches I've lain with in the past had no complaints, after all. Maybe it's not as big as some I've seen, but it's plenty for a human woman and Iolanthe's shock is doing wonders for my ego. It takes everything I have to resist the urge to stroke it in front of her fascinated eyes. "I am a big male. It stands to reason I should have a big cock."

Iolanthe just keeps staring at it, then leans over and peers in closer. If I close my eyes, I could almost imagine her breath against my skin and I bite back a groan of pleasure. "How in all the gods' names do you walk around with all that bobbing and sticking out? I have to bind my breasts so they don't wobble everywhere."

Well now. Those impressive breasts of hers are bound down? There's more to be seen? My cock pricks with want, and as she leans in, examining me closely, it makes me harder. "It…doesn't stick out all the time."

"Then why is it right now?"

She truly is innocent. "Because I'm aroused at the thought of you looking at me. I like it. And I like your curiosity, too."

Iolanthe glances up at me in surprise, a hint of a smile on her face. She bites her lip and then blurts out, "Can I touch it?'

"I would like nothing more," I rasp. "But just…just to learn. This is not about sex." At least, not in this moment. I feel someone owes her this. Someone should have taken a thirty-year-old woman aside and explained to her how things work, and part of me wants to punch her father for being such a gods-damned prick…and an awful part of me thrills that the only cock she's ever looked at is mine. Even so, it's clear that she'd be an eager partner.

So…I must be the one to set boundaries.

Iolanthe hesitantly reaches out her hand and then very carefully pets the head of my cock like she would a puppy. I'd laugh if it didn't feel so bloody amazing. Her eyes widen in surprise. "It's so soft."

I manage to grit out, "I assure you, it is not soft." Not when I feel as if I will explode if she asks to taste me. I've never wanted any touch as much as I want this woman—and she's to be my wife. Truly, the goddess Belara is smiling down upon me from somewhere.

Iolanthe chuckles. "No, your…privates are not soft. I meant your skin. It's very hot and yet so soft down here, and smooth. I don't know why it didn't occur to me that you would be." And her fingers graze the head of my cock again, producing a bead of wetness. "Is this…"

"My seed?" I manage to sound halfway sane, thank the gods, when all I want to do is shout for her to wrap those fingers around my shaft and pump. For her to take me into her mouth and taste me. I close my eyes and take another steeling breath. "Yes. When I push my cock inside you, I will eventually release my seed into your body. Sometimes it makes a child."

"Only sometimes?"

I nod. "A woman does not get pregnant every time a man mounts her."

"Oh. I didn't realize." Her cheeks flush and she strokes a fingertip down the length of my shaft, toward my heavy balls. "I thought a man only rutted his wife when he wished to produce a child."

"When we marry, I would like to touch you often. Not just to have a child. Just because it would bring you great pleasure, and I would like to give you that pleasure." I am babbling like the village fool, saying anything and everything as that soft, curious finger strokes my length. "There is a great deal of enjoyment to be had between man and wife. I would…I would like to share that with you, Iolanthe." I pause and then add, "If you'd let me, of course."

She bites her lip again and then straightens, withdrawing her hands and placing them on her cinched waist once more. "I don't think that's the kind of marriage my parents had," she confesses in a soft voice, and I can tell from her expression she doesn't quite believe I could be attracted to her. "Are you certain you wish to marry…me?"

Oh, I am certain. Now, more than ever, I want Iolanthe. Even if she wasn't a lord's daughter, I'd want her. I want those dark eyes, those freckles, and that soft, soft hand on my cock all over again. She's sealed her fate with her own curious touch, because orcs are known to be stubborn and single-minded. If her father changed his mind about our union, I'd show up on his doorstep to steal her tomorrow.

Like it or not, Iolanthe is mine from this moment on.

Iolanthe

Flustered, I try not to watch too closely as my husband-to-be hitches his pants back up around his waist and returns his belt to its position at his hips. I'm very grateful to him for treating me as an equal and showing me his body… and yet now I can't stop thinking about what this wedding will mean. He's going to put his hot, hard shaft between my thighs and fill me with his juices. I try to imagine our bodies fitting together, and it leaves me with a curious ache low in my belly. I flex my hand, thinking about how velvety his darkened green skin was on his cock, and how his breath hitched when I touched him.

I keep thinking about that hitch of breath even as he leads me out of the private study and back into the main hall…which seems to be rather empty. I glance around, but I do not see my father or his men. Agakor strides past me, a frown on his face as he notices the same. "Where is Lord Purnav? Where are his men?"

"Gone," says one of the men wearing an eyepatch. "They left with the bride-price and have already set off." His gaze flicks to me. "Said that if you'd compromised his daughter, she was yours now and he wouldn't take her back."

Compromised. Because I spent a short time alone with a half-orc man. I hate that he's right—no respectable lord would look upon me as a good candidate for a bride now. And…I did touch Agakor's privates. I'm ashamed of myself and humiliated at my situation. What if Agakor changes his mind? He doesn't have to marry me now, after all. He could refuse and send me back to my father…who wouldn't take me. I swallow hard, staring at the floor.

Agakor swears under his breath. "Selfish prick." Boots thud on the stone floor of the keep, and then Agakor touches under my chin with one finger. I glance up at him, trying to mask my hurt and probably failing miserably. His expression is soft as he gazes at me, his eyes kind. "Nothing has changed, Lady Iolanthe," he says, soft enough only for my ears. Louder, he continues, "I will be sleeping in the main hall tonight, and Lady Iolanthe shall take my chambers. Find her a chaperone, and tomorrow the first day of the wedding shall begin."

"Of course, Agakor," one of the men says, and heads out the door. The rest of the room stares at us, and I can feel the hot prickle of their eyes. I'm humiliated once more, the old, too-strapping daughter of a minor, poor lord. I'm not wanted. My father didn't even wait to count his gold, just raced back to his keep as if I'm a toothless nag he's glad to be getting rid of. Hot tears prick my eyes and I fight the feeling of worthlessness. All is not lost, I remind myself. Here, I will have a chance to be the wife of a lord, no matter how questionable. I might have children. I might—

Agakor moves in front of me, his ugly face troubled. He studies me for a quick moment and then takes my hand in his and kisses my knuckles, loudly and obnoxiously. "My lady, he is a fool. He might have a wagon full of gold, but I have the true treasure."

Everyone stares. I confess, I do, too. Not only because Agakor is clearly uncomfortable at playing the courtier, but…he's trying. Something tells me my hand is the only one he's ever kissed, and my heart melts a little. He wants me to feel welcome and lovely. He wants me to feel like he's being honored with marrying me, not that I'm a joke.

So I give him the world's smallest curtsy of acknowledgement and manage a smile.

For him.

The chaperone found for me is a wizened old woman named Turnip.

"I'm sorry, what did you say your name was again?" I ask politely as she's introduced.

She scratches the white cap atop her stringy gray hair. "M'called Turnip." Her chin lifts. "You need fresh clothes or somthin'?"

Agakor looks embarrassed as he ushers her towards me. I've been sitting at the table in the center of the great hall, picking at an overcooked dinner as the night wore on and we waited for someone to bring back a chaperone. "She's a washerwoman from the village," my husband-to-be explains. "I'm sorry. It was the best we could do under short notice." He rakes a hand through his thick hair, clearly agitated. "No one will come. I didn't think—"

"It's quite all right," I say, pasting a smile to my face. Turnip looks like she's led a hard life, her cheeks weathered and her mouth surrounded by lines. Perhaps she'll view her time with me as a vacation. "If Turnip is fine with being my companion for a few days, I'd love her company."

Turnip screws up her face at the sight of me. "Companion?"

"To a lady," Agakor says. "Just until we are married."

"She's the lady?" Turnip asks, scowling in my direction and displaying the two teeth she has left. "She ain't very dainty. Ladies are dainty."

I dig my fingers into my skirts. "My name is Lady Iolanthe of Purnav, Turnip. Pleased to meet you." I offer her my hand. "I am here to marry Lord Agakor."

"This 'un?" She thumbs a gesture at Agakor and then shakes her head at me. "Fool. Ain't you got eyes? He's a half-orc."

"Nevertheless," I say in my politest tone. "He is the lord of this keep and I am to be his wife, and so he is owed our respect."

"Hmph," is all Turnip says. "Show me my bed then."

Agakor steps forward. "Madam, the bed is for my bride-to-be." His expression looks as if he's trying to hide his amusement, even though his tone is grave, and it fills me with a surge of affection for him. "Her companion will sleep on a pallet upon the floor."

"Don't seem like a very good deal for me," Turnip grumbles.

I have to bite the inside of my cheek to keep from laughing. This is all very ludicrous and yet…surprisingly enjoyable. The food here is terrible, the keep dirty, but everyone is sassy and full of smiles. I try to think of such responses at my father's keep and cannot find one. Everyone there is somber and slightly sad, and the washerwomen flinch when they catch sight of my father for fear he'll yell at them.

There is promise here after all. My father has hurt me and humiliated me, and my new husband's home is a mess. But…a keep can be cleaned. A cook can be procured. A man that smiles when an old washerwoman berates him? That is a priceless find, half-orc or not. I'm smiling as I get to my feet. "I don't mind sleeping on the pallet. We must respect our elders, after all."

Turnip cackles. "Got yourself a smart one, Lord Orc. Even if she's as broad as a barn."

I flinch at her thoughtless words, but Agakor only turns his smile in my direction. "I like that she is tall and fit. What am I to do with a little mouse?" And the gaze he turns on me is clearly approving. I think about how I touched him earlier, and how velvety and hot his cock was, and how it jumped at my touch. My cheeks flame and I duck my head again, feeling shy but pleased.

We're led through the interior of the keep, and Agakor escorts me like a gentleman, my hand tucked into his thick arm. We head upstairs, toward Agakor's private quarters, and as we walk, I make mental notes of things that can be improved. There are lovely candle sconces on the walls, but they're covered in drips of wax and gutted, spent tapers. There's trash built up in the corners of every hall, but the keep itself seems to be of sturdy make, the stonework good. The halls are an excellent size, and there's a lovely window at the end of one that shows a pretty, stained-glass vision of the goddess Belara holding a dove. That has to be a sign, doesn't it?

Turnip is spry and seems to know the keep. She heads for a pair of doors on one side of the hall and pushes them open. "Taken the old lord's rooms for yourself, have you, Lord Orc?"

"Why not?" Agakor asks, glancing over at me. "I purchased the keep from him. I am the one in command here now."

I place a calm hand on his, to let him know I support him. And when Turnip steps inside, I gasp at the glimpse of the rooms before me. There's an enormous bed, sure. That's to be expected. But along one wall, there's a massive bookshelf filled with reading materials of all kinds—some scrolls, some leather-bound books, some simple sheaves of parchment tied with ribbon. With pure delight, I step forward and head unerringly for those shelves, pulling one book and then another from their home. "This…this is wonderful," I say, clutching a volume of Yshremi poetry to my breast. I turn wide eyes toward Agakor. "Are all these books yours?"

"They are. Do you read, then?"

My heart lightens. I can forgive my father's departure, or the fact that he didn't tell me my husband-to-be was a half-orc. I'm to live at a keep with books. So many books. "I love to read," I admit shyly. I'm almost reluctant to put the poetry volume down, I want it so badly. "Do you read, then?"

He shakes his head. "The books are spoils from a great many places, but I have not read a single one. It is something I should like to conquer."

"Perhaps I can help you with it," I offer. "Reading is wonderful."

Agakor grins at me, his eyes bright. "I should like that."

Before either of us can say anything else, Turnip moves to the bed and flings herself onto it. "We're sleeping, are we not?"

A short time later, Turnip snores loudly in the bed and I snuff out the candle next to my pallet, hugging the volume of poetry to my chest once more. I've stayed up late reading—I can't sleep anyhow. The blankets are soft and comfortable and of a fine make, and my head rests upon a thick goose-down pillow. More spoils, I suspect. I sit up in bed, the room dark, but I can see a gleam of light from under the bedroom door, and out there, a moving shadow. Agakor and his guards have set up sentries to ensure that Turnip and I are not disturbed. Oddly enough, I feel safe and comfortable, and it's not just thanks to Turnip's snoring.

Agakor has been kind. It's clear he's had a rougher past that he's moving beyond and is working to become a good lord of this land. While the keep is a little dirty, everyone seems happy and well-fed. And there are books, and…

And I think about how I touched his cock. I want to touch it again, to brush my hand over that velvet hardness and watch his reaction. It sends a thrilling prickle through my body and makes me breathless. I think about the marriage customs he mentioned. The Revealing of the Bride, as the Cyclopae call it. It seems both demeaning and exciting, a showing off of my body to my future husband so he's pleased with me. Normally I'd be revolted at the thought of letting a man see me naked, with my thick thighs and long legs and my heavy breasts. But Agakor says he likes all those things.

Unless…unless he's lying? The thought steals my breath away.

There's a flurry of footsteps outside of the doors, and the murmur of low voices. I could swear I hear Agakor, so I get to my feet, clutching my long, worn nightgown to my chest so it doesn't drag upon the floors. I creep forward and listen. It's thicker than I'd like, muffling their words, but I can still make them out when I press my ear to the door.

"…get some sleep, Agakor."

"I'll stay." His voice is so rich and smooth it makes my belly flutter. "She's my bride. Her safety is my responsibility."

"Can't believe her father abandoned her like that."

Agakor huffs. "Can't you? He doesn't give a shit about her welfare. All he wanted was my gold. That's fine. Let him leave her behind—it means he can't stop the wedding."

There's a pause, and then another voice asks, "This is your first time to get a look at her, innit? All the locals went on about Lord Purnav's massive daughter. What do you think of her, now that she's here?"

I bite the inside of my cheek so hard that I taste blood. I don't want to know. *I don't want to know.* What if he thinks I'm disgusting? How can I go through with the wedding if he does? How can I not, now that I've been abandoned by my father? Gods, I don't want to know.

Another pause, and my ears strain to hear Agakor's answer. "She's…breathtaking. I am well pleased."

Breathtaking?

I want to melt onto the floor into a puddle.

I'm...breathtaking to someone. For the first time in my life, I feel pretty and wanted. With a smile, I back away from the door and return to my pallet on the floor, tucking the blankets around me. I listen to the cacophony of Turnip's loud snoring and think about velvety green cocks and my upcoming marriage...and that I'm breathtaking.

I can't stop smiling.

Agakor

I don't see much of my bride the next day until the feast. There are a dozen things that must be done. Sentries are posted to the borders of my lands, and spies sent out to see what Lord Purnav is spending my coin on. There are weapon practices and hunters returning from the woods and a tax assessor from Adassia's capital on my doorstep. I'm so busy that I scarcely have time to breathe until Tindal, my second, grabs me by the collar and yanks me into the stables to change into my feast finery, and then we head back into the keep.

The moment we step inside, it's like I'm entering a different place.

The interior of the keep smells sweet. Pleasant. I see bundles of fresh greens placed at the end of each of the tables in the main hall, and there are fresh, new candles in all the sconces. The wax drippings have been scraped away, and the floor is clean. A new, impressive tapestry hangs just above the massive fireplace at the front of the hall, and the mountain of ashes is gone, replaced by a cheery fire. Near the hearth, the lord's table is set with two impressive-looking chairs and an equally impressive banquet spread before it.

I eye Tindal. He's full orc, from my father's clan, but good and trustworthy and *somewhat* civilized. He's a good arms-man and has an air of authority that keeps men in line…but I didn't think he was big on feasts. "This your doing?"

He shakes his head. "Your little bride-to-be marched into the kitchens at dawn and put everyone to work. If you don't like it, say the word and—"

"I like it," I interrupt before he can get the wrong idea. "I like it very much. I'm just surprised."

"Expected a fine lady to sit on her arse while we roll about in the muck, did you?" Tindal snorts at me, dusting a bit of lint off my tunic. "All them fine ladies run a good house."

"You an expert on fine human ladies?" I ask.

He smirks. "Some. My father used to steal 'em on the regular. Ransoms, you know. Easiest bit of coin you'll ever make. Sure did cry a lot, though." Tindal gives me a not-so-gentle push toward the center of the room. "Lord sits in his chair, remember?"

I grimace at the reminder. I don't feel like a lord. I know I'm in charge here, but even as I approach the lord's seat at the front of the room, near the fireplace, I'm reminded of all the sneers I received as a child, of the people that spat on me for being half-orc. The villagers that thought my mother was a whore and me less than dirt. I think of all those voices as I slowly approach the chair.

I've come a very long way from that scared, green-skinned lad. My skin might be a deeper gray-green now, and I might be muscled and tall enough that no one will think about spitting on me, but I don't feel like a noble either. But…that's why I'm marrying one, isn't it? I sit in my chair and try not to tug at the collar of my tunic. My neck is far too thick for the embroidery around the throat, and it pulls when I move. Looks nice, though.

I rub my mouth, suddenly nervous. There's no sign of my bride, and I'm starting to worry that she's run away in the night. But why clean the hall? Why—

Someone claps their hands together, starting a rhythmic beat. Others pick up the beat, adding in until the entire room is thundering with sound. My heart races and I cannot stop the grin that spreads across my face.

My bride is arriving for the first part of our marriage ceremony. The doors to my study open, and I jump to my feet, ready to get a look at my wife-to-be…only to catch sight of Turnip instead. She scowls at me and shoos the others away, and then a beautiful, tall creature steps out of the shadows and into the candlelight.

Breath escapes me.

Lady Iolanthe is stunning. Maybe not in the traditional ways humans value, but her skin is flawless, her freckles dancing by the candlelight as she steps forward. Her long, dark hair has been pulled into two thick braids that are knotted and encased in pretty chains. They dangle down her shoulders, brushing against her bosom and trailing over the front of her dress. It's a fine, beautiful dress, perfectly fitted to Iolanthe's form, and dips deep to show off her cleavage at the embroidered bosom, then cinches in to emphasize her waist before flaring out again. A thickly embroidered train sweeps across the floors as she moves forward, and my mouth goes dry. Her eyes are dark and shy, but she is smiling so brightly that it makes my chest ache.

"You look thunderstruck," Tindal murmurs. "Close your mouth."

I snap it shut. I just…cannot stop staring at the gorgeous creature before me. She has worn finery to her Cyclopae wedding ceremony, and while it makes her look incredible, it will just be ruined. Part of me wants to warn her, to tell her to go back and change. But her gaze flicks to mine, shyly, and I take in a deep, shuddering breath and know I will say no such thing.

Adjusting my tunic to hide the aching tent in my pants, I get to my feet once more and begin the formal words. "Have all seen my bride and judged her to be fair?" I call out.

"Aye," they call out, cheering and clapping.

Iolanthe just smiles and blushes, her fingers twisting in her skirts at the center of the room.

Now comes the hard part. "Display her before her groom and the gods," I cry, raising a goblet of wine into the air. "Let the Revealing of the Bride begin!"

I am watching Iolanthe with an intense gaze, and perhaps I'm the only one that sees the tiny shiver that she gives. Her face is flushed, the look on her face a mix of terror and excitement. Her eyes are glazed as the old washerwoman, Turnip, moves to her side and tears at one artfully sewn sleeve.

My soldiers go wild. They've heard of this tradition and have even seen it a few times before, but never a lady, and never their leader's mate.

Iolanthe flinches, and I force myself not to shove my way to the center of the room and rescue her. They will think there's something wrong with her, something I am hiding, and the last thing I need are more rumors in regard to my marriage. It takes everything I have (and Tindal's hand on my shoulder) to remain in place as Turnip ineffectively tears at Iolanthe's other sleeve. Normally a maiden would have two or three women stripping her bare, but my keep is full of soldiers and mercenaries. She only has Turnip, the most fragile, most cranky washerwoman I've ever met.

As I watch, Iolanthe taps a spot at the front of her bodice, and Turnip grabs the dress there. This time, when she yanks, the sound of fabric ripping is so loud that it echoes in the room, and another raucous cheer fills the hall. Iolanthe's dress falls to shreds at her feet and she stands timidly in front of me, waiting for judgment.

As if I could ever think she is anything less than perfect.

The freckles that cover her face disappear at her cleavage, leaving only soft-looking, unblemished flesh. Her breasts are much bigger than I anticipated, and I remember what she said about binding them under her clothes. They are heavy and full, her nipples tight as she is exposed to the air. Her hips are thick and flare out to long, strong legs and thick thighs, and undressed, she is every bit the strong, strapping maiden she was rumored to be.

I've never seen anything more beautiful.

Swallowing hard, Iolanthe keeps her hands at her side,

though her fingers clench and unclench. She moves slowly, turning and presenting her plump, rounded backside before facing me once more. Her chin lifts, and she's trembling, but she meets my gaze and waits.

"I find my bride pleasing," I manage in a hoarse voice.

Another roar goes up from the crowd, and the clapping and shouting is so loud I cannot hear myself think. I step forward, ripping my tunic off and moving to Iolanthe's side. My only thought is to cover her up, to make this better for her. I wanted to do this ceremony because as a male, it pleases me to think of my bride stripped bare in front of others, that I get to see her naked, lush body presented in front of me so others can see the bounty that will be mine. But the reality of it is as terrible as it is titillating. Iolanthe looks both faint and defiant, and I feel like a churlish ass for putting her through this.

I pull my tunic over her head and tug the length of it until she is completely covered. She pushes her hands through the sleeves, blushing, and then frees her braids, even as everyone continues to call and yell obscenities at us.

"W-what now, my lord?" Iolanthe asks, her hand going to my arm.

She looks far too good, slightly mussed and flushing and wearing only my tunic, and it's distracting. I adjust my stiff cock in my pants—which causes another round of laughter to rise from my men—and lead her over to the chairs waiting for us. "Now the wedding feast."

When she's seated, I grab Tindal's cloak and drape it over her legs, then take another cloak handed to me and bundle her in it. Iolanthe is covered from head to toe, her gaze downcast, but there's a hint of a smile to her mouth as if she's amused at my fussing. I glare at my men until they calm down, and with a quick signal of my hand, the feast is served.

The music starts. It's not great music—it's more fit for a campfire than a fine wedding—but the flutes and drummer are enthusiastic, and they're all we've got. Wine is poured into every cup, and trenchers of bread are passed around and filled with meat and vegetables. Hunks of cheese and bowls of nuts from the larder are brought to our table, along with cakes and pies of the likes I have never seen before. It all smells incredible, and I pick up one puffy, flaky pastry and sniff it. Gravy oozes out of the side and I take a bite, and it's the most delicious thing I've ever tasted. "This is amazing," I say, incredulous. "Who taught Cook to make these?"

"I did," Iolanthe says, adjusting the cloaks I've piled atop her. "I hope you are not offended that I stepped in to help organize your keep?"

Offended? I'm tempted to crawl under the table and kiss her large feet. "You are a wonder."

She looks pleased at my words, beaming at me. Her gaze flicks to the center of the room, where Turnip has picked up one of her discarded sleeves and waves it above her head in time to the music. Iolanthe leans toward me. "Are you…certain you are pleased?"

"More than pleased," I admit, taking another bite of savory pie. "Did it frighten you?"

"It wasn't my favorite," Iolanthe confesses, pulling the cloaks tighter around her. "But I suppose we are even now."

Even? I choke on a bite of pie, then thump my chest with my fist, because she's going to kill me. Now I can't stop thinking about Iolanthe's shy touches on my cock as she discovered it and petted it like a pup. I was not thinking of "even" as I showed her. I merely wished to ease her curiosity. "If tonight seemed offensive, tomorrow night shall be more to your liking."

She licks her lips, nervous. "Remind me what tomorrow is again?"

I grin at her, nearly beside myself with anticipation. "The Tasting of the Bride."

Iolanthe

I lie in bed, unable to sleep. My thoughts race from the day, and I can't concentrate on reading, even though I have a stack of Agakor's books at the side of my pallet. Turnip snores in bed, completely unbothered by the events of this evening, but I turn them over in my head again and again.

I wonder if it's wrong that I'm not more upset over the fact that I was just stripped naked in front of strangers. Should I be? I think of my sisters and how they'd have reacted. It's just that…I knew it was coming. I knew it was part of the ceremony, and that ceremony was important to Agakor. He needs a bride that is noble, but also one that is willing and understanding of his people's traditions. And I want to be a good wife. I know he's half-orc and I should find him repulsive, but he's kind to me, and he has books, and, well…I keep thinking about how he let me pet his private parts so I wouldn't be frightened.

I'd stayed up all night to loosen the seams along one side of my dress so it could be easily torn from my body. So the ceremony could be quick. And while it had been alarming and distressing, I'd watched Agakor's face as my body was revealed to him. The rapt look on his face at the sight of my naked body had been everything. Even though his men had hooted and called at me, he'd stared and stared and declared me pleasing. When he'd gotten to his feet, I'd noticed that the front of his pants was stiff and tented, and I'd thought about how he'd said he grew hard when he was aroused.

I'd done that to him.

The revealing was over quick enough—I'd stayed at Agakor's side for the rest of the feast, covered in cloaks as he'd fussed over me and offered me small tidbits to eat so I wouldn't have to reach across the table. For an ugly, hairy half-orc, he's…sweet. He's not even that ugly, not to me. His features are strong and not all that human, but he smiles a lot, and I like that.

Tomorrow is the Tasting of the Bride.

I twist my fingers in my nightgown, trying to imagine what that will be like. I'm still not entirely sure I understand what's going to happen. He said he's going to taste me, between my thighs, and he's supposed to please me there. That it has to do with some old Cyclopae legend. But no one's ever touched me there. Sometimes I experiment and touch myself, but I quickly stop because it seems…wrong. Like I'm doing something I shouldn't.

Tonight, I slide a hand under my nightgown and imagine his head there. I'm scandalously wet, and I worry that's a bad thing. My pulse feels fixed between my thighs, and I'm restless and breathless. I should have asked more questions about this next part of the ceremony. I should have asked for specifics. After all, what exactly *is* a "tasting"?

I see the movement of feet from underneath the door, the shadows shifting, and I wonder if Agakor is out there.

I wonder if he can run me through the ceremony in private, so there won't be any surprises. So I don't embarrass him or myself.

As I get up from the bed, Turnip snores again, rolling over in Agakor's thick blankets. I smooth my nightgown and then run a hand down my braid before moving to the door. Nervous, I crack it open, and there are two guards waiting just outside the door, both of them orcs. They slouch against the wall, but jerk to attention the moment I open the door.

I bite my lip and stand in the doorway, feeling a bit foolish. "Is Agakor nearby?"

"He just left," one says while the other eyes me warily. "I'll go fetch him."

"Oh, it's not necessary..." My words die as the orc trots off, heading down the hall in search of my bridegroom. This was poorly thought out, I realize, as the other orc smirks at me with a knowing look. "I just had a question for him."

"Sure," the other orc says, and keeps on grinning as if he knows exactly what's going through my mind.

Flustered, it's on the tip of my tongue to tell him that I've changed my mind and I don't need anything when Agakor appears down the hall. He strides toward my rooms, a worried expression on his face. His hand is on the knife sheathed at his belt, and he's still dressed in the tunic he wore earlier—a tunic I had Turnip send back to him once I retreated to my rooms after the feast. The collar is open and it's slightly wrinkled, but… he looks good. He looks better every time I see him, actually. I like his heavy, dark brows and his equally dark eyes. I like that wide, slashing mouth of his and the heavy jaw. All of him is commanding and strong and oddly appealing.

He turns those dark eyes to me as I stand timidly in the doorway of my room—his room, actually—and emotion flashes over his face. "You've changed your mind." Agakor states it flatly, as if it's a given. "You no longer wish to marry."

"What? N-no, that's not it at all." I want to tug on my braid or my clothes, a nervous habit, but I force myself to hold onto the door so I don't seem like a ridiculous twitchy fool. "I actually have questions about tomorrow. They can wait, of course. I'm sorry to get you up."

Before I can manage a polite smile and retreat, Agakor gives the two guards at the door a glance and then steps inside. "No one comes near here," he growls at them, taking my hand in his and leading me into the dark. "We won't be but a moment."

He leads me a few steps into the bedroom and doesn't release my hand. The door to the hall remains open, spilling some light into the otherwise dark room. Turnip doesn't stir, continuing to snore, and Agakor glances over at her, his face craggy in the thick shadows. "She's a deep sleeper."

"I think she drank a fair amount at dinner," I whisper. "Should I wake her?"

Agakor shakes his head and lifts my hand to his lips, pressing a light kiss on my knuckles. The broken tusk to one side of his mouth grazes my skin, but instead of alarming me, it sends a shiver through my belly. "Are you certain you still wish to marry?" When I nod, he brushes another kiss over my knuckles, and my nipples prick in response. "Then tell me what troubles you."

I'm distracted by his mouth on my knuckles. His lips feel soft and firm against my skin, and very warm. The caresses are distracting and making that strange heat pulse between my thighs again. "I…I don't know what to expect," I whisper to him, unable to take my eyes off of his mouth on my hand. "What is a bride tasting?"

"It's where I pleasure you," he murmurs, kissing my knuckles again. Something hot and wet grazes against my skin and I realize it's his tongue, and I suck in a breath.

"But how? Are you going to…bite me?"

He chuckles, the sound low and deep and makes my belly thrum with anticipation. "You don't know how? You can't guess?" When I shake my head, he presses soft kisses to my knuckles again. "Like this, love. How my mouth is on your hand? That's how it'll be on your cunt."

And he licks my knuckles once more.

I gasp, shocked and fascinated at the same time. "You…are you sure you wish to do that?"

"Oh, aye." Agakor brushes his lips over my skin. "I can think of little else. I want to brush your soft folds apart and then press my tongue to your seam, just like I'm doing right now." The tip of his tongue dips and presses between my knuckles, and it feels obscene and decadent at the same time. "Are you worried I won't make you feel good? Because an orc always makes sure his woman comes twice."

I shiver all over, fascinated at that big mouth on my hand, at the press of his tongue into my flesh. "I…see…"

He smiles over my hand and then brushes his thumb over my fingers. Funny how much bigger his hand is than mine. "I regret we cannot practice. I would love to touch you before the ceremony, but we're not supposed to be alone together."

"Right," I say faintly, not pulling my hand free. I can't stop staring at his sensual mouth as he continues to press tiny kisses to my hand. By all the gods, I feel hot and achy and feverish, yet I know I'm perfectly healthy. I lick my dry lips. "I'm so sorry to disturb you with my silly fears."

Agakor rubs my fingers again. "First, they are not silly fears. Your family has taught you nothing about the marriage bed, and even if they had, Cyclopae customs are not Adassian customs. And second, because it is you, it is never a bother." He gives me one last kiss on the back of my hand. "I'm just relieved you didn't have second thoughts about my ugly mug—"

"Never," I breathe, and then blush at how fervent I sound. "I gave my word."

"I don't want your word," he murmurs. "I want you willing and eager in my bed. All the agreements in the world matter nothing if you hate me for touching you."

"I don't hate it." The words feel as if they're being ripped from my throat, and my shyness wars with my need to tell him how I feel. "And I don't hate you. I want to be your wife."

He grins again, and the sight of it no longer alarms me. Instead, it fills me with yearning. "Until tomorrow, then, my pretty bride." He releases my hand, casts an amused look over at Turnip's still-snoring form, and then heads out the door. It closes after him, leaving me standing in the shadows in my nightgown, the place between my thighs throbbing.

I lift my knuckles to my mouth and press my tongue there, in the same spot where he touched me, but it doesn't feel the same. It's so much better when he does it...and I think about the times that I've furtively touched myself between my thighs. If that feels good when I do it, how much better will it be when Agakor touches me?

With an excited shiver, I return to my pallet and lie down. I don't sleep, though. Instead, I stare at the ceiling and try to think of things that need to be done around the keep, dishes for tomorrow night's dinner, and I rub my knuckles the entire time.

Agakor

I am a fool for insisting on the three days of the wedding in Cyclopae tradition.

If I had married her in the Adassian fashion, I could have simply bribed a priestess of Belara to show up at my keep. Throw a few coins at the townspeople to display my wealth, put on a feast for any that arrive, and have my pretty, blushing bride under me before the night is up. Instead, I must wait three full days, and pray that she doesn't change her mind.

Three days of a rock-hard cock and too-sensitive skin. Three days of forcing myself to stay busy because the sight of her fills me with lust. Three days in which I regret over and over again that I did not simply marry her quickly and efficiently in the Adassian way. If I had, she'd be under me even now, my face buried between her thighs as I teach her all the things that a married couple can do in bed together.

I am absolutely a fool.

When my scouts come back and tell me that Lord Purnav has been using my funds to buy the allegiance of every shield for sale in this end of the realm, I again, think that I am a fool. I should have just taken the girl for myself, kidnapped her from her father's keep and stolen her in the custom of my father's people. Orc men take the bride they want and then pay a penalty to the tribe if the union causes problems with peace. Given that orcs love to war, there's usually problems.

But I'd wanted to do this the human way. Make sure that everyone is pleased and all palms are appropriately greased.

"You think he's coming to war against me?" I ask Tindal and Jofeth, my master-at-arms. "Steal his fine daughter back?"

Jofeth snorts. "He doesn't want her back. He just wants your gold. It's more likely that he's figured out you're rich and wants to see what he can get away with."

I suspect they're right, but it bothers me. My inquisitive, brave Iolanthe deserves better than a father who's more interested in his horses and lording about the countryside than his family. Still, she's mine now.

Or she will be tomorrow night, when this ridiculous wedding I've insisted upon is finally completed.

Jofeth lifts his chin as he looks at me. "You look like you need to stab something. Want to spar until your wedding feast?"

"Lots of feasting tonight," Tindal adds slyly.

I just grin. I can't even deny it. I'm hungry to taste my bride.

I want to see how Iolanthe reacts to my mouth upon her. If she'll make those same fascinated, slightly shocked gasps she made last night when I deliberately tongued her hand. I can't wait. But until then… "Get your swords. I could use a good workout to take my mind off of things."

I sweat all afternoon. My men are well trained already, so the swordplay is skilled and intense. By the time the sun begins to set and the big, red moon comes out, I've soaked through my tunic. Tindal ushers me inside and I take a quick bath by the fireplace in his quarters, since the women have mine. I dress in my finery I've had put aside for this day…and I'm still sweating.

Gods, I should have known better than to give it my all this afternoon. Now I'm going to show up to taste my bride with a sweaty demeanor? Bad enough that I look more orc than human. My body seems determined to chase her away. I mop my brow again and again, but by the time I go out for the feast, I still feel sweaty and disheveled, and I worry she's going to take one look at me and bolt.

But when I sit down next to her, she gives me a shy smile and fusses with her clothing. She looks as delectable as ever, her hair piled atop her head and showing off a lovely neck and all of the freckles that dance across her skin. The dress she wears is tightly laced across the bodice, her magnificent breasts hidden underneath cinched layers. I think about those mouthwatering handfuls from yesterday, though, and know this is deceptive… and oddly enough, I like it. It's like a secret only for me.

Then again, I'd probably like it if she wore something with her tits spilling free to her navel, too. I'm a simple sort.

She leans over as I sit down next to her. "Is the tasting… before or after dinner?"

"After." I hope I finish sweating by then.

"Of course." Iolanthe bites her lip. "Not that I'm eager. I was simply curious—"

"I'd prefer you eager," I tell her, and when she blushes, smiling, it makes my cock hard. By all the gods, I'd rather just toss her over my shoulder and head to my bedroom and forget this Cyclopae wedding tradition. Truly, I'm an idiot. I grab my wine goblet and down a mouthful, or else I'm going to be a sweaty disaster before the meal is over. Just Iolanthe's nearness is enough to make me hunger for her.

I eat a few bites of everything, but I'm distracted. I can't drink vast quantities of wine because I want my senses to be alert for the upcoming tasting. I notice absently that the food is good—delicious, even—but I am paying far more attention to the woman at my side. I notice Iolanthe toys with the food on her plate and eats almost nothing. She drinks a great deal of wine, her hands shaking, and answers me with brief responses. She's nervous.

This feast feels like a farce. We're not eating. Why are we doing this when I could be between her legs already? Then again, I don't want to seem like an eager pup, out of control. I don't want to embarrass her. So I sit in my chair and try to concentrate on the fact that my men are enjoying the feast. If nothing else, they seem pleased at the largesse of the ceremony, and a contented soldier is a loyal soldier. It doesn't matter that my men are mercenaries or were once bandits or outcasts. I want them to know they have a place with me. That they can build a life here at my keep.

Just like I'm building a life with a new bride.

With that thought in mind, I get to my feet.

A cheer goes up from the crowd in the hall, ribald jokes filling the air. "Tasting," Tindal cries, making the two syllables a chant that's quickly picked up by the others until the entire keep seems to be shaking with shouts of "Tasting! Tasting!"

I hold my hands up, waiting for silence. I want to look over at Iolanthe, but I'm afraid if I do it'll just make things worse, so I keep my gaze focused ahead. When the crowd settles down, I speak out. "You all know the second part of the Cyclopae wedding traditions—the Tasting of the Bride." My men roar encouragement again, and I have to wait once more for them to quiet. "This ceremony will be performed in private. Where is my bride's chaperone?"

"I'll chaperone," calls out one of the mercenaries, leering.

I point at him. "You'll sit down and be quiet if you know what's good for you."

This brings another round of laughter. I cross my arms over my chest and give them my sternest look, and eventually the laughter dies down again. "Where is my bride's chaperone?" I ask again.

A loud, nasty belch echoes in the hall, and the old, withered woman—Turnip—steps forward. She wipes her mouth on her sleeve and gestures at me. "Let's get this shit over with."

In this moment, I truly, truly regret my choice of chaperones. How is it that no other woman will come to my keep? I watch as the laundress staggers out of the room, and nervous laughter erupts. I turn to my bride, finally, and I'm not surprised to see her face is pale. She gets to her feet and smooths her skirts, and then smooths them again.

And again.

I move to her side and take her hand before she can rub a hole into the cloth. Someone makes a lewd cheer and I pull her closer, ignoring them. "Do you need me to get you a better chaperone?" I ask. "Say the word and we will delay this for as long as you need."

My bride shakes her head and gives me a bright, brave smile. "I'm ready."

Iolanthe

Oh, goddess, am I ready for this?

My breath rasps quick and panicky in my lungs. I try to look calm, placing my hand on the arm he holds out for me. He leads me through the hall, shooting a sharp look at anyone that catcalls in our direction. I'm positive I'm shaking like a leaf, but I'm not entirely sure why. I'm not scared of Agakor. He's proven that he's kind, and tender. If this will hurt, I know he'll be gentle. Perhaps it's something else inside me that makes me shake. My belly quivers as we head down the hall and up the stairs. Two of his guards move behind us, and Turnip leads the way, a jug of cheap wine in her hands. It's like she refuses to leave the party behind, even now, and I'm not sure if I want to laugh or cry.

I think about Agakor, his hands on mine last night, his tongue pressing into the soft flesh between my knuckles. Did I interpret that wrong? I still feel that I don't know what I'm doing, and perhaps that's why I shiver with every step, and why I have to bite back a tiny moan at the sight of the bedroom doors. It's his room, the room Turnip and I have been staying in. The old washerwoman must not be as drunk as I thought, because when we step inside, I see that she's had candles put in all the sconces, and fresh bedding is on the large four-poster bed. My bed is rolled up and neatly tucked away into a corner. I didn't even think about this room today as I rushed about, working with the kitchen and the scullery men to ensure that the feast was handled and the keep was as tidy as it could be. I immersed myself in running things so I wouldn't dwell upon what was going to happen tonight, and I'm grateful to Turnip for handling things for me.

The two guards behind us shut the doors to the bedroom and stand in the hall. I'm left alone with Agakor and Turnip, and the very large bed. My face burns with embarrassment, and I feel so jittery my teeth feel as if they should be clacking together. It's only the hard press of my lips that keeps them from making noise, I suspect, as I stare at the massive bed. Agakor is silent and steady at my side, as always, but he says nothing, and I worry he's waiting for me to speak up.

If I had any words, they're trapped under the nervous knot in my throat. Mutely, I cling to Agakor's arm, waiting. What do I do now? Do I sit on the bed? Wait for him to take command? Throw my skirts up and say "Yes, please taste me now?"

After a moment more of silence in which I stare at the bed, Turnip sighs heavily and heads over to the stool and table set up at the far corner of the room. My new sewing projects are in a basket there, and she hefts her bottle of wine perilously close to delicate fabrics. "Look, are you two gonna do this or not?" She waves a hand at us. "I'll be here with my bottle. Just let me know when you're done with this nonsense."

I want to laugh, but my throat feels like it's closing in. The only sound that escapes is small and choked.

Agakor chuckles, though, and pats my hand. "Sorry if we're taking up your valuable time, Turnip." He looks over at me and winks. "We can get started if Lady Iolanthe is ready."

I manage a jerky nod. "Ready."

He gestures at the bed and I sit on the edge, feeling awkward. Yesterday, I knew the perfect gown to wear. Today, I wasn't certain how I should dress, so I wore a traditional Adassian gown, one of my favorites. The bodice is high and tight, my breasts flattened by the tight stays and lacings. My layers of skirts and the lower half of my chemise spill out at the waist, and I elected to wear nothing underneath. Bloomers seemed a silly choice when I'd just have to take them off again. I shift on my seat at the edge of the mattress, wondering if I should just haul my skirts over my head, or if he wishes to go under them. "How—how does this work?" I manage nervously. "Do I…"

I trail off, because I truly have no idea what to say.

Agakor notices my distress. He smiles at me, his big face creasing into that friendly look that I've come to delight in. He holds his hand out and I place mine in his. "No need to be worried," he murmurs in a low voice. "It's just me here with you."

I glance over at Turnip.

He shakes his head and reaches out, touching my chin and forcing me to look over at him again. "It's just me here with you," he murmurs again, words pointed. Our eyes meet, and I nod. I understand.

Agakor moves forward, lightly brushing his fingers along my jaw. "You need not worry. I will be nothing but gentle."

"I know that." I do, I truly do. He's been so kind. "I just…I still can't picture how this works."

"May I touch you? Show you?" His dark eyes search my face.

I nod. He has to touch me to get this underway, doesn't he? Else this marriage won't go forward, and my father will have to return my bride-price and everyone at home will starve…

Just the thought makes me panicky, and I hitch my skirts up, baring my legs. Everything bunches up at my waist, so I immediately lie back on the bed and haul my skirts up higher, presenting myself to him. I squeeze my eyes shut and clutch my gown against my midriff, my breathing shallow. Gods, why did I do my corset up so tight this day? I wanted my dress to have smooth lines, but now I cannot draw a deep breath, and I desperately need one.

It's utterly silent in the room. Agakor says nothing and I inwardly wince, wondering if he's finding me unappealing. I mentally go over the dark tuft of curls between my thighs, my long legs, my knees, my big feet, and I compare my form to that of my dainty sisters. But he saw me yesterday, didn't he? He said I was pleasing—

The bed creaks and then the mattress shifts, a heavy weight pressing down to the side. The big hand touches my face again. "Breathe, Iolanthe. Breathe."

I open my eyes and look up into his concerned face. His

fingers lightly trace my jaw, sending shivers through me.

"It's just us," he reminds me again, voice soft as he continues to touch my face. "There's no need to be nervous."

A tight laugh bubbles out of me. "You're not the one being tasted."

His eyes darken. "I can be, but not tonight." Before I can ask about that intriguing statement, he rubs his thumb across my chin and shakes his head. "Tonight is about pleasing the bride, so she knows her groom is the right one for her."

I manage a nod even as I gulp down air. "Very well."

"Can I loosen your corset for you? If you pass out, I'm afraid this will look badly on me." He gives me a wry grin.

I sit up on my elbows, reaching for the ties. Right. Loosening my corset sounds like a good idea.

Agakor puts a hand over mine, stopping me. "I want to do it. Tonight is about me pleasuring you."

Oh. I lie back again, my hand falling back to the skirts I have bunched up at my waist. I don't know what else to do with my hands so I just kind of clutch the fabric close as he leans over me. He's so big, I realize. Even with my height, Agakor is massive. His shoulders are broad and he's easily half a head taller than me. It shouldn't please me so much but it really, really does.

His hand drifts over my mouth, brushing my lips. "I know I'm not the most appealing to look at. Would you prefer I not kiss you?"

I open my mouth to respond, and my tongue brushes his fingertip. I immediately gasp, and he draws back a little, startled. It's like we're both on edge. But his skin was warm, and pleasant, and I suddenly want him to put his hand back again.

So I lick my lips and gaze up at him. "Please kiss me."

Agakor grins, the smile lighting up his craggy face, and for a moment, he's the handsomest thing I've ever seen. He settles down on the bed next to me, shoulder to shoulder, and I don't move. I just lie there and clutch my skirts to my waist like a madwoman and watch him. He reaches over and touches my cheek again, stroking it, and then leans in, brushing his lips over mine.

It's the first kiss I've had.

I've dreamed of having one, but never in my dreams did I imagine I'd be kissing a half-orc. That I'd be lying in bed with my skirts rucked up to my waist as tusks grazed my lips. But he smells good, and he's warm, and his mouth is so, so gentle on mine that some of my nervousness fades, and I press my lips back to his in the tiniest of return kisses. He kisses me again, clearly in no hurry to move away from my mouth, and his fingers stroke my cheek. He rubs his face against mine and then takes my lower lip and gently tugs on it with his teeth, sending a shiver through my body.

"Part your lips for me," he murmurs.

I do, and his tongue brushes into my mouth. I expected this, but knowing that it happens and feeling it happen are two different things. I've known that kisses involve tongue sometimes, but I didn't imagine it'd feel so…intense. That there's no intimacy quite like his tongue rubbing against mine, or that it'd make heat pool deep inside my belly.

He continues to kiss me, his tongue licking at me, our lips playing together, and his hand skims over my bared flesh below my skirts. I immediately freeze, all pleasure disappearing in a flash, replaced by uncertainty.

Agakor's big fingers stroke down my belly and part the folds between my thighs. He rubs lightly, and then his mouth flexes against mine as he grunts. "You're bone dry, love."

"Should I not be?" I whisper. Am I already doing something wrong?

He huffs in a quiet laugh. "It's not you. It's just me having far more confidence in my skills than I should." He kisses me on the mouth again. "Will you look at me?" I open my eyes and gaze up at him. His eyes are so very dark, his face so close to mine. "Are you frightened of me?"

I shake my head. There are a lot of things racing through my mind right now but fear isn't one of them. I'm anxious as a barn cat in a yard full of hounds. I feel exposed and vulnerable, and a little intimidated by what happens next, but I'm not afraid of Agakor. "I just don't know what to do," I confess. "When I was educated on my marriage duties, it was about how to properly run a keep and assist my husband with the books, not…this."

"Then let me educate you," he murmurs, and pulls my lower lip into his mouth again, tugging on it. It should feel odd to have someone sucking on your lip, but it sends little shivers through my body and I find it incredibly distracting. Almost as distracting as the hand still between my thighs, rubbing a finger up and down my slit. Agakor nibbles on my lower lip again. "I'm going to put my mouth on your cunt, like I put it on your hand last night. And I'm going to lick you everywhere and make sure that you come, twice, because that's how orcs are. We like to make sure that we're outperforming everyone else."

"I…see."

"It feels better if you're wet," he continues in that low, husky voice, his gaze pinning me in place even as one finger glides slowly up and down through my folds. "Normally I'd kiss you and work you with my mouth until you're soaked and your honey is all over my tongue, but if you think you can't get wet for me, that's all right, too. I have some oil I had brought for tonight, and I can use it if you'd rather."

I frown slightly. "But your mouth…"

Agakor grins down at me and gives me another kiss. I love that he's so free with his kissing. He kisses my mouth and then the tip of my nose, as if I'm precious to him, and it melts me. "The oil tastes fine. Not as fine as your cunt, but it doesn't matter. The object is to please you with my mouth, and I can't very well do that if you're dry, love. There's no shame in using a bit of something to slick you up. I promise it'll make you feel…so… good."

He punctuates the last three words with kisses and then removes his hand from between my thighs. He lifts his fingers that he had on my skin and licks the tips, then groans, closing his eyes. "Gods, woman. You taste amazing."

His words make me want to squirm like a puppy.

I'm breathless as he gets up from the bed and crosses the room. I sit up on my elbows, glancing over at Turnip. She's got her back to us, though, and drinks from her jug of wine as if nothing's going on. Agakor turns back to me, a tiny, tiny pot in his big hands. The front of his pants are tight, tented over his length, and I remember touching it. My insides clench at the memory of how he'd felt, and I bite the inside of my cheek, remaining still as he sits on the edge of the bed next to me. The need to pull down my skirts wars with the need to please him and do this ceremony right, so I watch him for cues and say nothing at all.

"I got this from the midwife in the village," he says. "I'm assured it's safe for a woman's body and will not cause any problems. She makes it for many of her customers, so I don't want you feeling as if there's something wrong. Understand?"

I nod. "Thank you."

His big black brows furrow. "For?"

"For thinking of me. Of my comfort." I manage a small smile.

Instead of smiling back, he just shakes his head slightly. "Sometimes I really do feel like a monster around you. You shouldn't be thanking your husband for thinking of your comfort. It should be his duty."

I flinch at his words. Do I truly make him feel that way? I'm ashamed, because would I have asked the same thing of one of my father's knights? Am I treating him differently? I consider this and then blurt out, "I'd be just as terrified right now if you were fully human, Agakor."

He gazes down at me and then grunts. "You're right. I'm just…tetchy about such things. Forgive me."

"As long as you forgive me as well. We're still learning each other." I give him a small smile. "We're bound to make mistakes."

"So we are. Lucky for you, I'm quite experienced in this next part. And you are incredibly beautiful, so this is a pleasure." Agakor leans in and kisses the tip of my nose and then pulls the stopper from the small pot. "Tell me if you get nervous."

"*Get* nervous?" I manage. "I've been so nervous all day I feel as if I'm going to snap like a twig."

He chuckles, dipping one big finger into the tiny pot. "Then let me take care of everything." He lifts his finger, and it gleams with oil in the candlelight of the bedroom. It's like he's presenting it to me, as if showing me what he's got on his skin…and I'm a little surprised when he leans down and gently presses that slicked finger to my mouth. "Taste."

A hot rush of arousal surges through me. I lick his fingertip, our eyes locked, and bright flavor unfurls on my tongue. It tastes like…berries. I taste him underneath, and on impulse, lick his fingertip a second time.

"Very good," he murmurs, rubbing his finger along my bottom lip. "I'm going to slick your pretty cunt and make it good and wet. Yes?"

"Yes," I whisper against his finger, and suck on the tip before he pulls it away.

He climbs off the bed, and the front of his pants strain with the sheer size of his cock. There's a wet spot on the front, and I think about the bead of wetness I'd seen when I petted him. It came out because he was so aroused, and I wish, suddenly, that he had his pants off so I could admire his body again. It was different, but I liked looking at him, so very, very much.

I'm so distracted with thoughts of Agakor taking his pants off and parading about our bedroom that when his warm hand touches my flesh again, I jump, a squeaking sound erupting from my throat.

"Did I startle you?" he asks, drawing back.

"I…it's okay."

He puts his hand between my thighs again, rubbing more of the oil between my legs, and it feels…all right, I guess? I haven't noticed a big difference other than his fingers glide through the folds a little quicker now instead of dry flesh rubbing against dry flesh. He removes his hand, coats his finger again, and then drags it through my slit.

A shiver ripples through me.

"I'm just going to touch you for now," he murmurs, moving to a table beside the bed and setting the pot down. "Get you used to my touch. Tell me if you want me to stop, all right? We'll take things slow."

"All right."

I try not to jump when he places that big, warm hand between my thighs again. His touch is startling—of course it is—but when he skims a hand up my thigh, it feels nice. Comforting. He rubs my leg, focusing on just brushing his hand over my skin and massaging my muscles. I gaze up at him, watching as he puts his other hand on my opposite thigh and does the same. I'm going to have oil up and down my legs, but I can't find it in me to mind. I'm too fascinated by the intent look on his face as he caresses me.

"I love how soft your skin is," he tells me as one big hand glides toward the apex of my thighs again. "I could just touch you for hours."

"Won't that make the guests nervous?" I ask, because I feel like I should say something, and not just lie here like a lump.

Agakor chuckles, and I feel it in my thighs, from his hands there. "They'll think I'm a madman if we return too soon. Don't worry about them." His fingers skim higher, teasing at the join of my legs, and then one finger slides up and down my slit.

I suck in a breath. That felt…intense.

He makes an "mmm" sound in his throat. "Better, I think. I'm going to touch you on your pretty cunt, now. Tell me to stop if you don't like it."

One finger delves deep, gliding up through my folds, and then rubs a little circle around the bud at the top, the one that's so damn sensitive I never touch it. Immediately, I cry out, trying to snap my thighs shut around his hand. His big body is in the way, though, and all I end up doing is squeezing him with my legs.

"Shh," he murmurs. "I know it feels like a lot, but it's supposed to feel good, too."

I pant, startled, and clutch at my skirts. They're so bunched up and knotted in my hands that they're going to be wrinkled beyond salvaging, but I can't find it in me to care. "It's…fine. I'm fine. Everything's fine."

To my surprise, he laughs. His fingers glide over that bit of flesh again, making my legs twitch despite my efforts to hold still. "If I'm doing it wrong, how do you make yourself come, love?"

I squirm against his hand, because he's talking to me in an incredibly sensible voice, and yet his fingers are gliding over that bit and I can't concentrate. It's like I need to come out of my own skin. I need to burst. Something. I pant like an animal, fighting not to push his hands away. "You're…not…doing it wrong," I manage. "Are you?"

His big hand stills, and for a moment I think he's stopping and…I don't know how I feel about that. My hips wriggle, and a frustrated sound escapes me. His grin splits wider, and then he drags his thumb over that bud again, and I whimper. "Have you ever made yourself come, Iolanthe?"

I bite my lip so hard that it stings. I don't know how to answer that. I know what he's asking, but is there something wrong with me if I say no? All my life, I slept with my sisters in the same bed with me, piled together. When they left to marry their husbands, the housekeeper moved into my room with me.

I've never had privacy to explore my body. I've read some books that hinted at lewd things that happen in the bedroom, but they referred to them as an explosion. A wondrous release. But right now, all it feels like is that he's tickling me to the point that I'm going to wriggle off the bed. "I…don't know what to do."

It comes out as a whine, and I'm immediately embarrassed. I grab those fistfuls of skirt and shove them over my face.

He laughs, the sound rumbling and deep, and hearing it fills me with an odd pleasure. I have to fight the urge to smile. "Don't be embarrassed, Iolanthe. Didn't your mother teach you?"

I peek out from under my skirts again, meeting his gaze. "She died when I was ten."

"Servants, then?" He watches me, his fingers gently brushing along the edge of one fold.

Reluctantly, I shake my head. "Ladies are supposed to be kept pure for their husbands. It wouldn't be their place."

"Mmm. Well, for this husband, I'm a little sad you've never gotten to pleasure yourself. You should indulge every now and then."

His hands are terribly distracting. His voice is reasonable, his words calm, but he keeps tracing and touching, his fingers gliding over my skin, and I have a difficult time concentrating. "We—we're going to be married. Why would I need to?"

Agakor clucks his tongue. "That's the wrong kind of thinking, love. You touch yourself because it feels good. You don't need my permission. Of course, I'll be happy to touch you as much as you want." He gives me a sly grin. "It'd be my pleasure." When I give him a jerky nod, he continues. "Since no one has educated you, let me tell you what's going to happen. Do you know what this little bud is?"

And he touches that tiny spot that's so sensitive. I bite back a whimper and shake my head. I've never named it. I've tried to ignore everything between my thighs, actually. I've always thought of it as married people's territory, and that it was off limits to me, as a maiden.

"This is your clit. Some women like a finger inside them, but most like for this little bit to be teased and sucked. How does it feel when I touch it?" He rubs his thumb against the skin hooding it, and I want to climb off the bed with all the sensation that ripples through me.

I arch, panting and squirming. "Like it's too much."

"It's supposed to feel like too much, love. You lie back and you chase that feeling, all right? It's leading you somewhere. You chase it, and you let me touch you, and you just enjoy." His voice is smooth, deep, hypnotic. Comforting. "I've got you. It's going to build and build, and it's going to keep feeling like too much, but you let it happen. I promise when you do go over the edge, it'll feel so good."

Right. Just lie back and let him touch me. He makes it sound so very easy, but he let me touch him, so I can do the same. I lick my lips—they still taste of oil and his kiss—and try to relax. Agakor watches me, his fingers skimming up and down my slicked folds before he moves back up to the bud—my clit—again. He rubs small circles around it, circles that make me twitchy and breathless, and his eyes are on me the entire time.

The strange, tense feelings intensify, and I whimper, my legs twitching.

"I've got you," he murmurs, and one big hand goes to the back of my thigh and pushes it back, toward my belly. It spreads me even wider, and as it does, his fingers feel more blatant, more obscene. My flesh starts making wet, slick sounds, and I'd be embarrassed, but he looks far too pleased. And it feels…good? I think it does. I shift my hips, desperately needing more pressure from those fingers, and when he finally gives it to me, my breath stutters. "That's it, Iolanthe," he tells me. "Chase that feeling. Follow it. It'll feel so good you'll wonder why you never did this before today."

I want to whine that I don't know what to do, but I also want to please him. On impulse, I rock my hips, and a small moan stutters out of me when it sends a surge of feeling through my lower half. Oh…that was nice.

"That's right, love. I've got you."

His fingers move ever so slightly faster as they rub that small bit between my thighs, and he watches me with such intensity that it sends shivers through me. I rock my hips again… and then again. Before I know what I'm doing, I'm rocking my hips in time with his fingers, making noises in my throat as I chase that building, escalating feeling. My pulse seems to be pounding right over the spot that he's rubbing, and it only adds to the sensations.

"Look at how pretty you are, sweet Iolanthe," Agakor growls, and his words send a thrill straight through me. "This pretty pink cunt all slick and glistening for me. It's just begging for my mouth, isn't it?"

I whimper, rocking harder against his hand. "Close," I manage to choke out. "I'm…I'm close?" Something feels as if it's about to happen. I'm both terrified and excited. My hands claw at the bodice of my dress, tearing into the seams as I try to grip at something. Anything. "Need…something."

"I know. Just keep chasing, love. I'm with you the whole time." He doesn't change his rhythm, just keeps touching me in the same maddening way. "I'm going to keep rubbing this pretty little clit of yours until you come all over my hands, all right? So you take your time. I'll be right here."

For some reason, knowing that I don't have to rush makes me feel…better? I can take as long as I want. I close my eyes, dragging my hands over my breasts, and for some reason, it feels good to grip them. It makes everything happening below my skirts feel that much more intense. I tease a finger over a nipple and my legs tighten, jerking. Agakor makes an encouraging sound, and I remember what he said. *Follow that feeling.* So I do. I touch my breast and rock against his hand, and it keeps building, and building, the strange, twisty need turning into this hot, wild pleasure. It's like I need more, more, more—

Everything in my body tenses and tightens. I cry out as the pleasure intensifies, and his fingers feel like too much. I jerk, but his hand on my thigh pins me in place, and those big, gentle, slick fingers keep rubbing and rubbing and rubbing and…

I burst. Everything seems to clench up in my body, and bursts. Hot pleasure bursts. The intensity bursts. My control bursts. So much pleasure. It fills me with wonder. This is what they mean when they say *they erupt.* This is what they mean when they say they *explode with bliss.* I get it now. A choked sound bursts from my throat, and then a warm, wet liquid bursts from my body below.

Immediately, all the pleasure dries up. Oh, by all the gods. Did I just *urinate* on him? Horrified, I try to wrestle free from his grip—

But Agakor makes a contented sound and rubs his fingers

through that wetness. "Look at how good you are, Iolanthe. That was perfection. How did it feel?"

I swallow hard, a little shy. "Is it…am I supposed to get wet like that?"

He nods, dragging those fingers through my folds. I'm so slick now that it makes wet, squelching sounds, but the awkward, cringing part of me is too dazed with pleasure to pull away, even when he pairs his fingers up and rubs them up and down my cunt, pausing lower and dipping into what must be my womb. "Every woman gets wet slightly differently, but the wetness is good. It means your body is readying you for my cock." He glances up at me. "But not tonight, though. Tonight, you get my mouth only."

"The tasting, right," I manage dreamily. My limbs feel liquid. Tired. I'm sated, and it's a curious, boneless feeling, interrupted only by the slight squirm I make when he touches my clit again. It feels like a lot there, suddenly. Like too much.

Agakor's hand pauses. He rubs my leg, and I dazedly realize he's leaning over me, and one ankle is on his shoulder. "Do you need a moment?"

I nod, breathing hard.

He gently sets my legs down and then climbs onto the bed, lying next to me. He props up on an elbow, his hand on his ear as he gazes down at me. "You're beautiful, you know that?"

I chuckle, because his hand is drifting down to my thigh, as if he can't resist touching me constantly. "I am many things, my lord, but I am not beautiful."

"Anyone who told you that is a fool, and they don't see you like I do." His fingers trail up and down the inside of my thigh, and I find myself spreading them, just a little, because his touch feels good. "I've never seen anything more gorgeous than you coming on my fingers."

Even though part of me wants to hide at his words, I smile instead. This is what happens between a husband and a wife, I'm realizing. And he's taking care with me to make sure I enjoy it. That I have pleasure. And oh, by Belara, was that pleasure. It was pleasure so great that for a moment, I lost control of my body. No wonder the books always mention such things when they speak of romance and love.

I've just met Agakor, but if he can make me feel like that, I can see falling in love easily.

I turn toward him, turning so I tuck myself against his chest. "Did I please you?"

"Beyond words."

I smile into his chest, and when he strokes my hair, I feel so, so good. Amazingly good. It's incredible, really. All the tension I've felt over the last few days has drained out of me, and my legs feel as soft and boneless as uncooked dough. He rubs my back, and as I lie there, I become vaguely aware of something hard pressing against my leg.

It's him. His cock. It's erect and stabbing, even through his pants. And realizing how aroused he is makes me want to do something about it. I want to make him feel as good as he made me feel. "What about you?" I ask. "Can I touch you and make you burst?"

From across the room, someone clears their throat.

Turnip. She's listening in. My face heats immediately and I want the floor to swallow me up.

Agakor goes still at Turnip's reminder, too. He chuckles, stroking my hair again. "Not tonight, love. Tonight is all about you. That's how the ceremony works."

"I see." A smile touches my lips when he rubs his hand down my thigh. They're enormous, his hands. Not just from his orc heritage, I think. HIs mother must have been a large woman as well, because Agakor stands a head taller than all his men, orc or human. He's big enough that he makes me feel positively dainty in his arms, and I try to imagine him with someone as small and fragile as my sisters and I can't. He said he wanted someone tall that he wouldn't break…and I definitely fit that bill. I snuggle closer to him, pleased. "So…what now?"

He chuckles again, rubbing my thigh. "Love, that was just the warm-up. I haven't tasted you yet. Once you've caught your breath, we'll begin again."

I get to do that again? That incredibly confusing, delicious tensing that builds until everything inside me bursts and leaves me sated? I'm excited. "I'm ready now."

Agakor grins down at me. "My little maiden's eager for more? That pleases me."

Agakor

Iolanthe is shy, just like any sheltered virgin would be. I know that, and yet when she gives me an eager look and says she's ready to go again, my heart swells with pride and affection. I knew this lovely little human would be the perfect wife for me the moment she petted my cock and looked upon it with such interest, instead of skittering away like the virgin she is. She might be sheltered, but she's curious and eager, and those are the best traits in a new bride, I decide.

She's no longer scared. Her face is flushed, her eyes glazed from the pleasure I just gave her as she rocked against my greased-up hand. Just a short time ago she was timid and worried, but now that I've shown her what can happen, she looks dreamy and sweet, and when I settle my hips between her thighs, she obediently hikes her skirts and spreads them wider for me, showing me her pale flesh, gleaming with the oil I've rubbed into her skin. The curls that hide her pretty cunt are wet with both oil and her release, and my mouth waters at the sight.

I rest my hands on her hips and when she looks at me with dark, trusting eyes, I hike her higher on the bed, just enough that she's not on the edge, her legs dangling over. Now she's fully on the bed, enough that her heels can dig into the mattress—or my back, if she wants to throw them over my shoulders. I lean in, resting my elbows on the bed, and slide my arms under her thighs, spreading them apart and settling my bulk between them. "I'll go slow," I promise her. "So there won't be any surprises."

"I trust you, Agakor."

Such a sweet thing, to hear those words. I even love the shy, wondrous tone she says them in. Gods, if Lord Purnav knew what a prize he was giving me, I'd have had to pay him twice as much for her hand…and I'd have willingly done so. Iolanthe is sheer perfection in a bride. No man—human or orc—is luckier than me.

I nuzzle at the inside of one thigh, brushing her soft skin with my lips and tusks. She tastes sweet, like the oil, but there's a hint of salt that coats her skin that reminds me that she's wet from other reasons as well. I rub my face against her leg, fascinated with how soft she is. "When a man tastes his bride, he puts his mouth on her, like I did with your knuckles. Do you remember?"

She makes a soft whimpering sound and shifts her legs. "I do."

"If I do something you don't like, tell me, yes? But my goal is to get you to chase that feeling again. That it's going to build up in your belly and—"

"Lower," she blurts.

I pause.

"It's lower," she tells me, and I can practically feel her embarrassment. Her hand steals down between her thighs, and she pats the mound so tantalizingly close to my mouth. "When it builds, it's here."

I lean in and kiss the hand charmingly hiding her from my gaze. Her fingers twitch, and she caresses my face before withdrawing. "It's going to build here, then," I correct, and press another kiss, this time to her mound. "And it's going to feel good when you burst again. Just let it happen, but if you get scared or if something doesn't feel right, you tell me, yes? I'm right here with you, and there's nothing wrong with taking it slower if we need to."

"I'm fine," Iolanthe promises. Her hand lifts, and she hesitates, then reaches out and brushes my hair back from my forehead, then skims along my cheek. As if she…likes touching me. As if she can't resist. My heart aches in my chest.

The luckiest. That's who I am.

"I'm going to taste you now," I tell her, and turn my face to press a kiss against her hand. "Any time you want me to stop, just say so, or tug on my hair if you don't have the words. All right? If you don't like it, we won't continue." I flick my tongue against her palm, loving the little surprised gasp she makes. "But I think you'll like it."

Iolanthe nods, and I can feel her body tense underneath me. That's the last thing I want, so I turn back to pressing kisses against her thighs, stroking her skin with one hand as I tug the other leg over my shoulder. When she no longer looks as if she's about to bolt, I move in and press a kiss to that damp mound of hers.

She sucks in a breath.

"It's just my mouth," I remind her, kissing again. "You squirmed all over my hand and I made you feel good. My mouth will, too. There's nothing here I haven't seen or touched already. And if you get wet, sloppy wet, that's even better. I want that, Iolanthe."

The breath shudders out of her, and I can sense she's trying to relax. Her legs twitch, and I rub a hand over one thigh framing my ear. Her hands are back in her dress, clutching it into fists, but that's all right. As long as she stays with me, mentally, and doesn't panic, she can tear that dress into shreds for all I care.

I kiss her mound again…and then dip my tongue deeper, brushing against her clit.

Iolanthe gasps, her hands spasming.

"It's just a kiss," I murmur. "Just my mouth. I'm going to make you feel good with it. You know that, right?"

"Y-yes."

So I "kiss" her again, repeating the action. She trembles slightly, but her thighs part just a little more, and I'm filled with triumph. My brave, brave lady wants this. I press deeper, dragging my tongue over her clit, and her body trembles. "You taste so sweet."

"I-it's the oil."

Startled, I lift my head and look up at her. "What?"

"The oil," she repeats, dazed. "The oil tastes sweet."

I chuckle. "You think this pretty cunt of yours can't taste sweeter than that?" I reach over one thigh and use my fingers to spread the pink folds open for my hungry mouth and then give her an obscenely bold lick. "Delicious."

Iolanthe makes a whimpering sound. My cock is agonizingly hard, but I love this. I love getting this response from her. I love how this is all new and yet somehow, she's not afraid. She's experiencing it all with me, willing to spread her thighs and let me touch and taste her as I please. Such a good, sweet woman—and she'll be an even sweeter wife. Of that, I have no doubts.

I lick her again, and I can taste a hint of the oil, but more than that, I can taste Iolanthe. The musky arousal that coats her flesh. I'm not just saying things to placate her—the taste of her on my tongue is mouthwatering, better than any dessert. I lick her again, taking my time and dragging my tongue over every bit of that exposed pink flesh, until she's squirming underneath me. "Such a pretty, tasty cunt," I murmur. "I could lick you like this for hours and never get enough."

A low moan escapes her. She squirms a bit when my tongue grazes her clit again, and I suspect she's sensitive after already coming once. I won't be able to feast on her for hours, then. I need to make her feel good, to leave her dazed and sated and pleased with my performance, so the ceremony can continue, and when we go to bed tomorrow night as husband and wife, she'll be eager for my touches.

Just imagining Iolanthe with her hands on my cock again, that inquisitive, enthusiastic look on her face, is enough to make me nearly lose control. I close my eyes, my breathing ragged as I try to control myself. My cock feels as if it's pulsing in my pants, and I'm a breath away from spending myself like an unschooled boy. I have to focus. Concentrate.

When I've nearly got myself under control again, a hand brushes against my hair. It's Iolanthe, but she's not asking me to stop. She's just…touching me. As if she can't get enough of me.

It makes me wild with hunger. I bury my face in her sweet cunt, licking and tasting ravenously. She cries out in surprise and then makes little noises of pleasure when I find her clit and suck on the tiny bud of it. Her thighs tremble against me, and I tease her with my tongue and my lips, all pretense of taking my time and going slow having vanished as quickly as my control. My mouth is hot and fierce on her clit, and as I work it, I press a finger at the entrance to her body. It's slick and wet, hot and ready for my cock, and I groan against her flesh. By all the gods, she's perfection.

I slowly sink a finger inside her, and Iolanthe cries out. This time, instead of her fisting her dress, she buries her fingers in my hair and twists, pulling as I suck on her clit.

I lift my head, panting. "Should I stop?"

"No! Keep going! I'm so close!" She tugs on my head, desperate. "More…more of your mouth!"

I groan again, going back down on her. I love the quake of her hips that moves in time with my mouth, and I gently drag my finger in and out of her virgin channel. She's tight, but pulsing with heat and wetness, and I want to make this good for her. I don't add more fingers or seek out the spot on the inside of her wall that will make her turn inside out with pleasure. I'll save that for tomorrow, so I don't overwhelm her.

Iolanthe rocks against my face, the breath hissing out of her as she builds toward her climax. Her body tenses against me, the noises she makes more urgent, and when her cunt quivers around my gliding finger, I know she's desperately close. I want to talk her through it, to tell her what a sweet, good wife she's going to be, but I can't lift my mouth. I keep going, moving my tongue in the same rhythm I've been using and never letting up, no matter how much she pulls on my hair.

"Ah!"

The startled, sharp cry is the only warning I get before my face is flooded with her release. With a growl of pleasure, I lap at her, pleasuring her as she quakes and trembles with her orgasm, her channel squeezing around my finger. She writhes under me as the climax goes on, and when she's finally spent, her hands drop from my hair as if she's a puppet with cut strings, and she goes limp. I lift my head, looking up at her, and wipe my wet mouth. "Iolanthe?"

"Mmm?" Her tone is dreamy and soft. One tired hand reaches up to brush over my lips, touching my broken tusk, and her face is flushed red with exertion, her eyes dark. "Agakor… that was…"

I grunt when she trails off. It was, indeed. I shift my body, entirely unsurprised to find that at some point I came all over my pants. Probably when she climaxed. I was so focused on her need that I lost control, and now my pants are wet and sticking to my cock. Tindal is going to laugh his ass off at me…but I can't find it in me to care. "Did I please you, my bride?"

Iolanthe manages a huffed laugh. "Oh gods, yes. Yes, you did."

From the corner of the room, Turnip belches. "I guess that's my cue." She gets to her feet, heading for the doors. I'd nearly forgotten that the chaperone was there, I was so wrapped up in Iolanthe and her pleasure. I can tell my bride thought the same, because she jerks away from me, shoving her skirts hastily back down her legs just as the washerwoman flings the doors to the hall open. "We have a well-pleased lady," old Turnip bellows. "He made her scream like a banshee. Twice, even!"

A cheer goes up from down the hall, and the sound that escapes Iolanthe could be a laugh or a whimper. Maybe both.

Iolanthe

I block out most of the rest of the night.

I know this is Cyclopae tradition, so I ignore the catcalls and smirking looks. I sit back down at the front of the room as the feast goes on, and try not to blush too much as Agakor hands me sweet tidbits to eat. He's got a knowing expression on his face, and I catch myself staring at his mouth in between bites of food. I can't stop thinking about what we just did. How good it felt.

How I want to do it again.

How I want to do the same to *him*.

I'm pretty sure if my father had known about the bridal

tasting, and the bridal revealing, he would have been angry. Insulted. He'd have viewed it as a slight against our house and his name. Maybe stripping me naked and making Agakor judge me was definitely one-sided in his favor, but the tasting was entirely in my favor, wasn't it? I could have said I was displeased with his performance and things would have been called off. Turnip makes sure to tell everyone how much I cried out while he "dove between my skirts" and the looks the rough men shoot Agakor are full of envy, not mocking.

It's an odd, absurd ceremony—for me to reassure everyone that yes, Agakor pleased me well. Yes, he pleased me twice, as a good orc should.

I drink copious amounts of wine until I head to bed. Agakor leads me to my rooms, kisses my hand, and tells me how much he can't wait for tomorrow, for our wedding to be finalized. It makes heat pool between my thighs again, and this time, I know what that heat is for, and I whimper. Am I little embarrassed as Turnip changes the sheets on the big bed before she lies down? Of course. But when we both settle in to sleep, I'm wide awake. I think about Agakor and his mouth. Agakor and the way he held me as he pleasured me. Agakor and the way his hands skimmed along the insides of my thighs, and his mouth…

I touch myself quietly between my legs and I'm not surprised to see that I'm wet again. I move my hand away, breathless, and try to sleep. I can't, though. I keep thinking about Agakor and his smile.

Funny how I thought he was so ugly just a few short days ago. Now I can't wait to see him smile at me again.

The next morning, I dress myself and fix my hair. There are no ladies to help me with this, but I'm used to doing it on my own. My father has slowly whittled down his keep's servant staff over time to save money, and so I've learned to handle my grooming myself. Other ladies have a dozen maids to help them but…other ladies aren't marrying a half-orc warlord, so there's that. Turnip isn't a great chaperone, either. This morning, she's clutching her head and moaning about how much it pains her. I don't snipe that she shouldn't have drunk so much alcohol. I'm mostly just happy to have the company as I head down the stairs, eager and breathless to see my new husband-to-be this morning.

A lady should keep her composure, I remind myself as we head toward the main hall. I can't seem too excited to see Agakor, especially after last night, or the rumors will go wild and the mocking will never cease. It's just…now I'm truly excited for the wedding. This has gone from a daughter's duty to me anticipating our wedding night, and I'm pretty sure my face will be red all day long. I don't care, though. I'm happy, and I'm excited, and for the first time in a very long time, I'm looking forward to the future.

The great hall is empty, though. Yesterday morning, it was full of soldiers eating their breakfast before heading off for their duties, and I'd gotten to see Agakor in passing. I've woken up even earlier today in the hopes that we'd have more than just a brief moment to talk, but it seems it's not to be. There are a few young boys (both orc and human) clearing dishes from the hall, and I head toward the kitchens, trying to hide my disappointment.

"Good morning, Grundar," I call out as I enter the busy kitchens. Here, at least, there are signs of life. More boys scurry about in the kitchens, bringing in dirty dishes, washing pans, sweeping, and another helper pulls a large tray of freshly baked meat pies out of the oven and sets them down on a table near me. The kitchens are clean and neat, run by another elderly half-orc with an ugly face and a foul demeanor. I've decided I'm going to win him over, though, and I've showed up every morning to discuss menus with Grundar and get his input. He tolerates me and scowls the whole time, but he does what I ask, which is really all I can hope for. "How are you this morning?"

"Alive," he snaps, scrubbing an enormous pot. "What do you want?"

I ignore his surly tone. Perhaps it's cultural. "I wished to discuss what would be made for the wedding feast tonight. I assume there's another feast?"

"Day three, innit?" he says, as if I have no clue about my own wedding.

"That is correct." I beam at him. "And since this is the last official wedding feast and you've done such a lovely job the last two days with preparing the dishes I've asked for, I wondered if we might make tonight's fare a nod to my husband's heritage?"

"Eh?"

"Perhaps traditional orc dishes?" I clasp my hands at the waist of my gown. "I confess I don't know what those are, but I'd love to honor Agakor's family with them."

He shakes his head, chuckling. "You don't wanna do that."

"Why not?"

Grundar picks up a wooden spoon and then reaches past me and swats. I jump in surprise, turning to see Turnip holding her hand, a stolen meat pie shoved into her mouth. "Them's for the feast later," he tells her with a growl. "You don't get to eat them."

"I'm the Lady Rolandee's maid," she sneers at him. "That means I outrank you."

"My name is Iolanthe," I correct gently.

Turnip shrugs. Grundar snorts.

I decide to ignore that—all of it—and focus on the task at hand. The feast. "Why would we not wish a traditional orc dish?" I ask again. "Please educate me."

"Pine needles," Grundar says.

"Pine needles?" I echo, confused.

"Orc dishes are made with lots of pine needles," he agrees, giving one last shake of the wooden spoon at Turnip's direction before focusing on me. "Not much grows up high in the mountains, save for pine trees and moss. You want to taste an orc dish, it involves lots of meat and pine needles. They've got a strong, sharp flavor, which is good because orcs don't have very sensitive tongues." Grundar gives me a sly look. "Probably lucky that Agakor's a half-orc, eh?"

My face feels like it's on fire. "Perhaps let us do one or two dishes in the traditional orc manner and the rest as I outlined yesterday," I decide, ignoring the innuendo. "Do you have the supplies you need for the feast or is there anything you require?"

"Good here," he tells me, gesturing at the kitchen helpers racing about behind him. "Lots of meat, veg, and one of the boys is off to the village to get another bag of flour. Should be fine."

I linger, smiling at him. "Lovely. You're doing a wonderful job, Grundar. And speaking of Agakor..." My face feels even hotter as the old half-orc gives me a knowing smirk. "Have you seen him this morning?"

The cook picks up a canister of spices and turns his back to me, grabbing a handful and tossing them onto the carcass of a freshly killed deer. "Some trouble in town. He'll be back in time for the ceremony, don't you worry. I don't think anything could keep him out of your skirts tonight."

Turnip just snorts.

I'm really, really going to have to get used to the frank talk of these men if I'm going to live here. "Is there trouble in town often?"

Grundar gives me an odd look.

Is there some sort of issue I'm unaware of, I wonder? When he doesn't explain, I murmur something about checking on the progress in the main hall and exit the busy kitchens. We head out into the main part of the keep again, the only sound that of Turnip licking her fingers. "Do you know where Agakor's feast tunic is, Turnip? I think the collar was bothering him and I'd like to fix it before tonight."

She points to the laundry station at the far end of the courtyard, and I follow her over, trying not to think about "trouble in town." What could it possibly be?

Agakor

He's raising an army," the blacksmith tells me when I ride into town, my men at my back.

"Lord Purnav?" I ask, surprised. I still hand over the coin to the blacksmith, who's paid to keep me abreast of everything that goes on in Cragshold's adjacent town, Darkshire. "You're joking."

The blacksmith shakes his head, big arms crossed over his chest. "He sends riders into town when you're not here, looking to hire every mercenary or anyone that can carry a shield. No word on what he's preparing his army for, but rumor has it that he's planning to attack someone that stole something from him." The blacksmith lifts his chin in my direction. "I think it's you."

"I've stolen nothing from him."

"We both know that. He's telling these fools what they want to hear. You and I both know it's just an excuse."

I grunt. I knew he'd try something. It was a gamble, of course. Lord Pissant is the cheapest lordling in all of Adassia. I knew if I showed him what sort of wealth I have, it'd be a risk that he'd turn right back around and rob me. Of course, I'd been hoping to be wrong about him—that he'd be pleased his daughter was marrying someone who could take care of her, no matter his heritage, and we'd settle in to married life. It's not to be, of course. Because I'm half-orc, he thinks I'm less than him, and so do most humans. It'll be no big deal for them to rob me and raid my keep, because they don't think I belong there anyhow. It doesn't matter that I purchased the keep fair and square. It won't matter if I'm a good lord or not. They see a half-orc and they assume I'm a wild monster from the mountains, like my father's tribe.

It's infuriating, but not surprising. I offer the blacksmith coins for his information. "You have my thanks."

The man holds up his hand. "Keep it. I get plenty of business from you and your men, and everyone is always respectful and pays on time. I have no quarrel with you. If anything, I'm surprised so many are flocking to Lord Pissant, because he's well-known to be cheap."

He might be cheap, but he's fully human. Sometimes that's all that matters. I don't say this aloud, though. "Let me know if you learn anything else I should be concerned about."

"Will do." The blacksmith grins at me. "And congratulations

on the bride. She's a big, strapping one, aye?"

"She's magnificent," I tell him proudly. "A bride fit for a king."

"And nothing like her father," he adds in amusement.

There is that. My Iolanthe is as different as night and day when it comes to her father, and I couldn't be more relieved.

I linger in town, drinking an ale at the tavern and getting more information from my sources. Everyone talks about the mercenaries Lord Pissant is hiring, and how he's telling them he needs them for a "brief raid." I'm not too worried—my men are well-trained, and the mercenaries in town won't fight hard for someone like him. He thinks he'll be able to take over my keep with little effort, and his arrogance will be his downfall. My biggest concern is that my bride will be upset that her father and her new husband are at war. Will she pick me over him? Doubtful. She's only known me for a few days and has been his daughter all her life. The thought of Iolanthe choosing him over me is a depressing one, but realistic.

No one chooses a half-orc when there are any other options.

When I head out of town with my soldiers, a group of men meet us at the crossroads. The leader moves toward my mount, and I can see his armor is battered and used, weapons strapped to his back. He calls out to me, "You the half-orc lord?"

"Do you see any others around this town?" I say, amused. "What do you want?"

He eyes me, calculating. "Lord Pissant's raising an army against you. Me and my men here were interested in his coin until we heard he was coming against you. Your men all say you're fair and you pay on time. Ain't nobody says that about Lord Pissant. Wanted to see if you'd be interested in hiring us, instead."

"I'm celebrating my wedding," I say, choosing my words carefully. "But a man such as me can always use a few more loyal guards. You're welcome to join us. My second will be in charge of payment."

The men exchange looks, and I see them nodding. I don't blame them. Back when I hired my sword out for coin, it was important to be paid well, but it was more important to work for someone trustworthy. Too many of these lords think a sellsword is beneath them, and because of that, they short their pay, or don't pay at all. Reputation is everything amongst mercenaries, and mine is saving me right now. "We'll be joining you," the leader says, and then adds, "Lord Pissant says you're holding his daughter against her will, and he's going to be rescuing her."

Sigh. Of course he did. "Lord Pissant was paid an enormous bride-price for the honor of marrying his eldest daughter. My wedding to Lady Iolanthe will be finalized tonight. If Lord Pissant thinks his daughter shouldn't be marrying a half-orc, he shouldn't have been so quick to take my coin. He was willing to sell her, and I bought her hand in marriage."

The men nod. "We thought it might be something like that. It'll be his word against yours, though."

"So it is." I meet their gazes calmly. "And as I said, tonight is the wedding, and Lady Iolanthe has put a great deal of effort into getting things running smoothly. I won't have her upset by anyone, most of all her father."

The leader grins at me. "Strange day when a half-orc lord is the reliable one, eh?"

Strange indeed. I gesture to my men that we should ride on back to Cragshold Keep, and I'm not surprised that all of the mercenary band falls into place behind, joining us. If Lord Pissant tries something tonight, before I can truly marry Iolanthe, I'm going to murder him with my own green hands.

Iolanthe

It doesn't feel real, this wedding, until Belara's priest is brought into the keep and seated at a place of honor near the fire. Suddenly everything is *too* real, and my nervousness reaches a fever pitch. I race back to my room to spend the short time before the dinner feast and ceremony fussing over my hair and dress. I eye my reflection in the beaten copper mirror that appeared yesterday, smoothing a stray strand of hair into my intricate braid.

Tonight, I'll be a married woman. Tonight, I'll be in Agakor's bed.

A shiver of excitement curls up my spine. I thought I'd be

tired today considering I haven't slept much in the last few days. There's far too many things going on for me to relax enough to drift off to sleep. But just like the day before, I'm full of energy and excitement. I'm ready to marry. I'm ready to spend the evening in bed with my husband. I'm ready for…everything. I pinch my cheeks and bite my lips to plump them, then peer into the mirror to see the results.

I fuss and primp because I want to be as beautiful as possible for when I appear downstairs. I want Agakor's eyes to light up at the sight of me. I want my husband to think me lovely. Music starts downstairs—the drumming, rowdy beats that the mercenaries prefer. It's not what I expected with a wedding, but then again, I didn't expect to get married. I decide I like it. It's a little wild and uncouth, like our marriage. Scents drift up from downstairs, and I know they'll be coming to retrieve me soon. I bite my lips again and cinch my bodice a little tighter so my breasts are flattened enough to make a smooth form under my dress. When Turnip finally arrives, my lips feel bee-stung, my bodice is so tight I can scarcely breathe, and I'm brimming with excitement. I clasp my hands in front of my waist, do my best to look serene, and follow her down the stairs.

The moment I step through the doors in the great hall, a cheer goes up. A blush stains my cheeks, but I can't maintain my serene appearance. A smile tugs at my mouth, and when I see Agakor standing in the center of the room, in front of Belara's priest, I smile even wider. By the time I reach his side, I'm grinning like a fool. He smiles back at me, his tusks moving, and he looks handsome. So handsome. Not in a conventional way, of course, but I can't stop staring at him. The deep blue tunic I altered to fit his thick neck isn't entirely buttoned up, the neck loose and slightly rakish-looking. He wears a finely tooled leather belt at the hips, a heavy money-pouch hanging from it, and his dark hair is swept back behind the points of his long ears. His dark eyes are bright as they focus on me, though, and I feel like the prettiest woman in the realm when he looks at me.

Agakor holds a hand out, and I place mine in his. His hand is big, his palm slightly rough, but it feels so right. I step up next to him, and we both tower over the smaller priest of Belara, but Agakor is a full head taller than me and I still feel dainty at his side.

"You're beautiful," he murmurs as I step close.

I just smile again, and in this moment, I don't think I've ever been happier. I squeeze his fingers, because I don't know the words to say to convey my happiness. Today is my wedding day. I'm marrying a lord who is kind, encourages me to read his books…and licked between my thighs for an endless amount of time last night just to pleasure me. I feel blessed.

And when he lifts my hand to his lips and kisses it, his tongue brushing between my knuckles in a silent reminder, I feel blessed *and* aroused.

Agakor lowers my hand and then looks around the room. The music dies, and the murmurs of the crowd do, as well. Everyone is silent, waiting for the ceremony to begin, waiting for Agakor to bribe the priest of Belara, as is tradition. "I have called Belara's faithful to be with us today," my husband-to-be announces, and unhooks the money pouch from his belt. He holds it up in the air for everyone to see, and it's the largest blessing bribe I've ever seen. The bride and groom are supposed to be favored by the goddess depending on how much they spend (for Belara loves wealth as much as she loves beauty) and I'm a little stunned at the bulge of that sack. I suspect the priest is, too, because he looks awed as it's handed over to him. "I ask the goddess's favor so I may be joined in marriage to Lady Iolanthe of Purnav."

"Belara is honored by your generosity," the priest says formally. It's a rote response—Belara is always honored, even if those marrying can only hand over a single coin instead of dozens—hundreds—but I'm still thrilled by his words. He gestures for us to stand closer together. "Join hands so I may begin the rites of matrimony."

Agakor holds out both his hands to me, and I place mine in his. We face each other, and my shyness grows. He watches me with such intensity, as if devouring the sight of me, and it makes my breath catch. Or maybe it's just how tight my corset is. His thumb brushes over the back of my hand, and new, fresh heat pools between my thighs—

The doors of the great hall burst open and one of the guards rushes in. "My lord! Trouble!"

Agakor's jaw clenches. Reluctantly, he looks away from me and back at the soldier. "What now? I'm in the midst of my wedding."

The man jogs forward, and I see he's wearing one of the blue sashes at his waist—one that I've been told denotes loyalty to Agakor and not a mercenary here for coin. He strides toward us, glancing at me before stopping in front of my almost-husband. He lowers his voice. "A band of orcs on horseback are heading this way from the north, my lord. Rumor is they've come from the mountains and are charging this way. Shall I send outriders out to intercept them?"

My almost-husband groans. He releases my hand and rubs

his face, his expression tired. "Damn his timing."

"What is it?" I ask quietly. I'm aware of everyone in the hall staring at us, watching. Their ears are probably straining to overhear our conversation. "What's wrong?"

"Nothing's wrong, save that our marriage must wait a little longer." Agakor grips my shoulders and sighs. "It seems my father is on his way to join us."

His…father?

Iolanthe

I'm not sure what I expected Agakor's father to be like. Perhaps like my husband-to-be, with a calm, amused demeanor and a steady, quiet confidence. Mudag is the opposite of all of that. He's slightly taller than his son, with thick, wild black hair. His tusks are bigger, too, jutting so far across his face they're practically poking at his nose. Unlike Agakor's thick, solid build, Mudag is lean and rangy. He's all muscle, but it's ropy and rawboned instead of bulging. He wears a kilt made of skins, a necklace full of (what I hope are) animal teeth, and his hair is studded with flowers, and his belt is covered in them.

And he smells like a garden.

Heavily.

I swallow hard, trying not to be alarmed at the overly-perfumed scent of my soon-to-be father-in-law as he approaches with his men. Agakor leans in, my hand still tucked protectively in his arm. "That scent is the blooms," he murmurs. "Orcs use it to hide their scents from predators."

"Predators?" I ask politely.

"Owlbears, mountain naga, griffons." He shrugs. "Other orcs. Humans."

Right. "It sounds like a dangerous place."

"Which is why I'm here in Adassia," he agrees, grinning down at me. "Don't be alarmed by Father. He's harmless."

He doesn't look all that harmless, but then again, neither does Agakor and I'm growing fonder of him by the day. So I smile brightly and remain at Agakor's side as the band of orcs approaches, my eyes watering from their scents.

"Looks like we arrived just in time," Mudag says loudly, coming to a stop in front of us. Since the orc party was arriving, our ceremony was delayed and we moved to stand in the courtyard. Agakor said it was so if there was a mess, it wouldn't get on the clean floors. I had no idea what he was talking about, but gazing at Mudag's flower-covered garments and grime-caked boots, I'm starting to get an idea. The orc straightens to his full height, glaring down at me, and a few bright petals flutter to the floor.. "This the human?"

"Aye," Agakor says cheerfully. "This is my bride-to-be. Her name is Iolanthe."

My insides quiver with terror but I somehow keep smiling even as Mudag fixes his terrifying stare on me. "Pleased to meet you, er, Mudag." I have no idea how to address an orc, and

I hope I did so properly. Agakor has said before that he's not a lord, so I don't call Mudag one either. "You are just in time for the ceremony's completion."

He bares his teeth at Agakor as if grossly displeased. "A *human* wedding?"

"Cyclopae traditions," he reassures his father.

Mudag grunts, as if grudgingly giving his approval. "Well, now that I'm here, you can marry her in orc tradition as well. You'll have to wait a few days, but we can have the feast at least." He nods at us as if it's all decided.

Another wedding? Oh, by all the gods, am I going to have to get naked in front of everyone again? I shoot Agakor a panicked look. "Orc tradition?"

My husband-to-be is grimacing. "We don't have to—"

"You have to," Mudag bellows, leaning into his son's face and eyeing him balefully. Agakor ignores his father's mood, but the look he gives me is downright apologetic. Mudag is worked up, though. He points a stout green finger at me. "It must be the night of the full moon, with Belara's red eye upon you. My son will steal his mate away."

I relax. After the titillations of the Cyclopae marriage, being stolen away sounds normal. "That doesn't seem so bad."

Mudag lunges toward me, forcing me to leap backward. "He shall whack you over the head with the ceremonial club—"

"Sorry, what?" I must have misheard.

"The ceremonial club," Mudag continues. "He will strike you with it and knock you out so he can steal you away."

I blink at him in shock. "You did that to Agakor's mother?"

Mudag scratches at his chin. "Of course. She wouldn't stop fighting me otherwise."

"I don't think an orc wedding is a good idea," Agakor begins.

His father ignores him, his focus on me. "The next night, the chosen bride must try to escape her new husband, or else she's deemed weak."

I'd want to escape someone that clubbed me over the head, so I understand that part of the ceremony very well. "And after that?"

Mudag shrugs. "Once she's been sufficiently tamed, the chief will declare her a worthy bride." He leans in and winks at me, becoming almost cheerful. "I'm the chief, so just put up a good fight. Make my son work for it."

Oh dear.

He claps an awkward Agakor on the shoulder. "Not to worry, my son. She looks like a fine-sized lass, able to take a good clubbing."

I don't know whether to laugh or to cry. It *sounds* like a compliment. Poor Agakor looks frustrated as his father strolls toward the keep, eyeing it as if checking to see if it passes inspection. He leans in and rubs a dirty finger over a scratch on the heavy wooden doors, frowning to himself. Taking their cue from their leader, the other orcs stream inside, leaving me in the courtyard with Agakor and his amused guardsmen.

Agakor sighs heavily, running a hand down his face and pulling at his lower lip. "My father's timing leaves much to be desired. I'm sorry about this. You know I would never club you over the head."

He sounds extremely offended on my behalf. My lips twitching, I offer, "You'd club me somewhere else, then? Perhaps a shoulder?"

"No clubbing anywhere." Agakor gives me an exasperated

look that manages to be tinged with fondness. "Woman, you will be the death of me. I've been agonizing over having to wait three days to make you mine and now you want to do an orkish ceremony?"

Oh. How is it that this man is so damned sweet? How does he make me yearn for the marriage bed so dearly when a few days ago I was terrified of marrying someone as fearsome looking as him? I move forward and press my hand to the front of his tunic, smoothing the fine embroidery I added late last night, because I wanted him to look fancy in front of everyone. "Don't you want to be married in the way of your father's people?"

He leans in, giving me a lascivious look. "I *want* to be between your thighs."

My face heats. "I want that, too."

Agakor bites back the low groan building in his chest and glances around at the courtyard. "Two more days until the full moon. I must be three kinds of a fool to even consider such a thing." He rubs his knuckles up and down my sleeve. "I wanted you in my bed tonight. Is that greedy of me?"

I bite my lip. "I could still be in your bed tonight," I whisper. "We could sneak out and see each other. Touch each other."

He groans this time, loudly. "Iolanthe. How did I get lucky enough to win you?"

"You paid a lot of coin to my father? Is that luck?"

The look he gives me is downright pleased. "That he accepted the offer of a half-orc to marry his beloved daughter? I do consider that luck."

Oh. Does he think my father valued me? If only he knew the truth. My father saw me as a pawn to be used to marry off, and the moment I grew too tall and plain to be useful, he was done with me. I bite back a grimace. "Agakor, I'm afraid he might have made you think I'm more precious to him than I am. My father was glad to be rid of me. To him, I'm a burden." I pat the embroidery on his chest again. "Now I'm *your* burden."

Agakor doesn't look convinced, though. He frowns down at me as if the words I'm saying don't quite register. "Your father is mounting an army to steal you back, Iolanthe. I didn't want to worry you, but it's true. He's hiring every mercenary in the area and I suspect he'll be coming here soon and demanding your return."

That does not sound like my father. I shake my head. "If he's coming here, it's for one reason only, and it's not me. It's your money, Agakor. Your coin. He knows you're rich and probably thinks he can take it from you with a big enough force."

"Perhaps." He seems skeptical.

"I've known him for thirty years," I say, my tone light. "Trust me in that I know his motivations."

"You might know his motivations, but you do not understand your own value," he says, taking my hand from his chest and kissing my fingertips. "I am disappointed that we must endure another marriage ceremony. I was selfishly hoping to have you in my bed tonight."

My cheeks get hot. I glance around the courtyard. It's emptying out, all the arriving orcs and Agakor's men heading inside to eat the wedding feast for the wedding that's no longer happening today. "Would anyone notice if we went missing? Maybe we can steal away for a few minutes." I feel like a tart for suggesting it, but the idea is such an enticing one I can't help myself. I've been looking forward to the marriage bed, too. "Perhaps I can feign illness and you'll have to kiss me better."

He nips at my fingertips, the look on his face heated. "It wouldn't be proper. You're a lady, Iolanthe."

I don't want to be a lady right now, though. I want to be his wife. I want him to touch me. I shake my head. "I am going to have a headache in about two hours," I tell him carefully. "And I am going to pick up a book and hide in your study because the crowd will be too much for me." I give him a meaningful look. "I don't think anyone would notice if you left a few minutes later and joined me."

Agakor's gaze practically smolders as he stares down at me. "Do you mean to seduce me, Iolanthe?"

Do I? "I honestly haven't thought that far ahead," I confess. "But I thought maybe we could share a few kisses and touch each other…while we're waiting for our new marriage ceremony. Is that so wrong?"

He kisses my fingertips again. "Woman. You will absolutely be the death of me." He hesitates a moment and then says, "The solar. Second floor. Read your book there."

I nod. The solar it is.

We head back inside, my hand primly resting on Agakor's sleeve, as if he's a great lord and I'm his lady. Our chairs are still at the front of the hall, so I sit down while Agakor addresses his men—and the visiting orcs—and explains the change in plans. After our union has been sanctified by the orc leader, the ferociously grinning Mudag, the vows will be spoken in front of Belara's priest. Until then, I will remain a maiden.

There's a lot of disappointed catcalls and hooting at that, but I suspect no one's more disappointed than me. Tonight I was going to share my quarters with my husband…and now I must share it with Turnip once more. Grimacing, I sip at the wine and rub my temples, play-acting at a headache. It doesn't take much effort to "act." The orc tribe from the mountains is loud and noisy and reeks of flowers. I thought Agakor's men were boisterous, but Mudag's warriors put them to shame. Every word is shouted, every step is stomped, every dish is banged on the table, and they drink and carouse and have a delightful time. The poor flowers in their belts and in their hair fall everywhere and get crushed underfoot, and the smell just gets stronger as the night goes on. I'm a little shocked by their boisterousness at first, but it's all good-natured. They seem happy, so I don't mind the sound.

Of course, I pretend that I *do*.

Clutching at my head, I soon excuse myself, saying that I'm retiring to bed early. Turnip gets up from her spot and huffs with annoyance. She doesn't want to leave the party with me but does her job as chaperone. I ignore her grumping until we return to "our" quarters, and then I pick up one of the books beside my bed. "You know what? I'm not ready to go to sleep yet. I think I'll head to the solar and read for a bit."

She looks at me like I'm crazy. "What am I supposed to do? Watch you read?"

"No, of course not," I say, soothing. "Why don't you go back down to the party?" I gesture at the guards at the end of the hall. "It'll be fine. I'm just going to hide and read and then go to bed."

If I was expecting Turnip to argue with me, I'm mistaken. She brightens, her lined face creasing into a grin. With a jaunty nod, she turns and races back down the hall toward the stairs, and I want to laugh at how quick she's moving. Boy, Turnip really does love a party, even if it's full of orcs. Amused, I clutch the book to my chest and head for the solar, shutting the doors behind me.

The solar is always the lady's private room in a keep. My sisters and I spent a lot of time sewing and reading in the solar back at Rockmourn Keep, and I remember how my mother used to love to sit at the window and gaze out at the courtyard below, watching the goings-on. Ours was a large, comfortable room with a big window to sew by, and tables for ladies to sit at and work on projects. I remember my mother's loom, and the unfinished tapestries that lay about, the musical instruments for idle hands to play. This room is nothing like that. This solar has been long abandoned, no craft projects waiting for their owners. There's a small table to hold a candle or two, but the loom in the corner is empty, and the window seats lonely with disuse. Even the small, comfortable pillows I expect to see scattered about a lady's solar are missing. Whoever had this place before Agakor ransacked it. Sad.

I glance around at the empty room, wondering how Agakor is possibly going to sneak past his guards at the end of the hall. There's no other way into the solar. But maybe he intends for his men to see that he's here with me? Maybe they'll keep his secrets? I wish I knew. I find a striker and light a candle, but the room remains as shadowy as ever. It's dark outside and the moonlight isn't angled to illuminate the room through the window. Anxious, I sit at the window seat…and cough. It's dusty here. It's clear no lady has been in this room since the last one left, and I haven't had a chance to have the servants sent here to clean up yet. I fan my hand in front of my face, waiting for the dust to settle. From here, there's a good view of the muddy courtyard below, and I see a few torches moving back and forth, probably our guests getting situated for the night.

There's a creak behind me, the groan of a door opening, and I jump to my feet.

To my surprise, the door to the solar is closed, but I could have sworn I'd heard someone come in. "Hello?"

"Iolanthe?" The hushed voice is Agakor, but it's not coming from the direction of the doors, but the far wall, thick in the shadows.

"Where are you?" I whisper, moving over to pick up the candle I'd set on a nearby table. "How did you get in?"

He emerges from the shadows, his craggy face ghoulish in the candlelight. He grins down at me, and even though he's hideous, my heart melts. "Secret passage. Only a few know about its existence. This way we can meet and your reputation will be intact."

Like I give a damn about my reputation. We're to be married in a few days' time. I set down the candle again, and when he takes a step forward, I fling myself into his arms.

Agakor makes a sound of surprise, but then his arms go around my waist and he's kissing me. His tusks brush against my lips and it feels strange, but it also feels good. It feels like him. I let out a little sound of contentment as I wrap my arms around his neck and give myself over to his mouth. I kiss him with quick, frantic nips, as if we're going to be caught and pulled apart. "How long do we have?"

"How long do you want?" he asks, his hands roaming over my waist as he kisses me back. "What is it you want to do?"

"Everything," I tell him eagerly.

He groans, the sound turning into a chuckle. "My sweet, eager bride. I would love to thoroughly debauch you right here and now, but you deserve better for your first time. Let's just enjoy each other for a bit, shall we? Can I make you feel good? Like I did last night?"

When his mouth was between my thighs? I shiver with excitement. "You want to do that again?"

"My mouth has watered all day just imagining it."

"What about you? What pleasure do you get if we do that?"

He chuckles again. "You don't think it's pleasure enough?" His big hand skims down my skirts and squeezes one cheek of my backside. "You don't think I get intense enjoyment out of licking you and watching you squirm on my tongue?"

I'm panting at the thought. "I loved it. I want to do it again."

"Excellent. I like having a lusty wife," he tells me, hauling me up against him and leading me to the solar window.

A new thought occurs to me. If he puts his mouth between my thighs, can I do the same to him? I remember how he showed me his cock so I wouldn't be afraid, and how hot and velvety he felt. "Can I touch you again? Between your legs?"

He groans. "I'm not sure that's a good idea."

But the more I think about it, the more excited I get. I know all about my body—I'm far more curious to learn his. "You don't want me to touch you?"

My disappointment must be evident. Agakor's breathing becomes ragged and he rubs my arm. "Love, of course I do. I nearly came when you touched me before. But I thought you wanted me to pleasure you."

"I do," I tell him, breathless. "I liked it! But I want to touch you. You gave me pleasure last night. Can I do the same for you?"

The sound he makes is pained. "If I didn't know your father better, I'd say you're too good to be true."

I'm stung at this and draw back. I feel as if I've crossed some line that I didn't know existed, and I've been rebuffed. It hurts. "Oh? Should I not have asked?"

He hurriedly takes me in his arms again, pressing sweet kisses to my face. "That's not it at all, sweetheart. Gods, you think I wouldn't want that? It's just that we have to steal our time together. Wouldn't you rather me pleasure you?"

"But touching you is a pleasure for me," I say softly. "And I want to learn what pleases you, too."

Agakor makes a sound that might be laughter, might be a huff. Either way, he sounds both exasperated and amused at the same time. "If you truly wish to, Iolanthe, I won't protest. But know that I won't require any such thing of you in our marriage bed. I just want you happy and comfortable with my touch."

I smile at his shadowed face. "That's what I want for you, too." I bite my lip, practically beside myself with anticipation. "So…may I touch you?"

"As if I can deny you anything?" He takes my hands in his and glances around the solar. I have no furniture in here yet, other than the tiny table that holds the candle, but the window seat has cushions on it. Old, dusty cushions, but still cushions. His gaze moves over it and then he nods to himself, leading me to the seat and sits carefully on the edge of one. His feet are braced on the floor and he watches me, his expression guarded. Does he think I'll be bad at touching him?

I aim to show him that I can be a good wife in this aspect,

too. Eagerly, I reach for his belt at the same time he does, and he stops in surprise. Chuckling, I flick his hands aside. "This is my turn. Let me do it."

"I had no idea you'd be so eager to touch an orc," he muses, letting his hands fall to his sides.

"I'm eager to touch my husband," I correct, tugging at the knot of his belt and loosening it from the ring. It slithers free and I pull it from his waist, tossing it aside. His tunic is longer, reaching mid-thigh and covered with thickly crusted embroidery, as befitting a wealthy bridegroom. It looked nice at the altar, but right now I wish he was wearing a shorter tunic so I could just shove it up and have my fill. Carefully, I fold the tunic upward and tuck it around his hips, so as not to wrinkle it, and I could swear Agakor makes another one of those amused huffing sounds. "You'll want to look nice for our next ceremony," I remind him. "We can't wrinkle or stain things."

"Gods help me, I'm not sure how many more ceremonies I can take." He sounds hoarse, his hand reaching up to stroke my braid. "I'm ready for you to be mine."

His words send a thrill through me, as does the large bulge between his thighs. I'm excited to see his cock again, to see what touches he likes. Tugging at the drawstring to his pants, I loosen them and pull the material down, and his length practically springs free. Oh. It's just as big as I remember, too. I gasp with pleasure at the sight of him, immediately reaching out to touch once more. My fingers skim down the length of his cock, and he feels just as warm and velvety to the touch as before. It's such a pleasure to caress him that I sigh, trailing my fingers over him.

Agakor's cock twitches under my touch, and I notice that

he's gone very still beneath me. I realize that I'm practically hovering over him, my other hand pressing on his thigh. I'm probably pushing on him uncomfortably. "Oh. My apologies. Is there a better way to do this? Should I be sitting?"

The muffled sound he makes is pained. As I watch, fascinated, he reaches into his pants and pulls himself completely free, his sac nestling against the material of his clothing even as his shaft juts out toward me. "Some females—ah, *ladies*—get on their knees."

"I can do that," I tell him eagerly, and drop down onto my knees on the hard wooden floor.

"Wait," he says, and leans forward. "Here." He plucks one of the cushions off the window seat and drops it between his thighs, and somehow I'm paying less attention to the cloud of dust that puffs up this time. I'm too fascinated by the bob and weave of his cock as he moves. It's...hypnotic.

I move forward onto the cushion, unable to take my gaze off of his cock. My hands creep onto his knees and I gaze at him, reverent. "Have you had many ladies touch you between your thighs before?"

"I...don't know if I should answer that, Iolanthe." At his tight voice, I glance up, and he grimaces, his face twisting. "I just...I never expected to have a wife, much less a lady. So I played around with tavern wenches that would have me, and the occasional whore when no one would. But it's been a long time since I've done even that. There's no woman in my life but you."

"And Turnip."

He snorts with amusement. "I'm trying to forget that one."

I smile up at him. Hearing about his past doesn't bother me.

It's in the past, like he said. And in a strange way, I understand. I never thought I'd have a husband, so I haven't prepared myself at all for what a marriage entails. Of course he wouldn't think of a bride. Most of Adassia still thinks orcs are legends, mountain beasts in stories told to frighten children. I never thought I'd marry, much less marry an orc. "From this day forward it's only me, though, right?"

Agakor gazes down at me in surprise. "Gods. Yes, Iolanthe. Only you. I can't believe you'd have to ask. After touching you, you've ruined me for all other women." He reaches down and caresses my cheek. "And our marriage vows are sacred. I'll cleave to you and you cleave to me."

I lean into his touch, feeling warm and desired. "I just wanted to make sure. Some lords have a wife for show and a mistress for fun. I…don't think I'd like that."

"No mistresses. No lovers. No one but you." His fervent words sound beautiful to my ears.

Beaming, I impulsively lean in and kiss the head of his cock. After all, it *is* right there.

He sucks in a breath, his big body going still.

"Was that wrong?" I ask timidly. I lick my lips, because the tip of him was wet, and the salty flavor begs to be tasted. It's not the most pleasant of tastes, but it's fascinating in how sharp it is, as if it's conveying to me with its boldness just how strong his need is.

"Not wrong," he reassures me, tone brusque. "Felt good. I was just…surprised. You sure you want to do this?"

Is he going to keep asking me? Do ladies not want to do this to their husbands? Or is it because he's half-orc and thinks he doesn't deserve my touch? Either way, I can't help but think of how good he was with me in our bed last night. How he made me feel so good and so comfortable before putting his mouth on me, and how incredible it had felt.

Of course I want to do the same for him. It's exciting to think that I could give him even half as much pleasure as he gave me.

"I want to do this," I reassure him. Reaching out, I touch a fingertip to the head of his cock again. Agakor relaxes a bit, caressing my face as I touch him. I want to look at his cock, but the way he's devouring me with his eyes makes it hard to look away from him. "You'd tell me if something I did wasn't okay?"

This time he chuckles, his thumb stroking over my cheek. "I don't think you could do anything that wasn't okay with me. Even biting. Sometimes orcs like it rough."

Biting? I blink down at his cock. "I'm not sure I should bite you."

"Of course not, sweet." He gives me a rueful smile. "I'm just talking in general. Hells, I'm just rambling because I can't concentrate on anything but your hand on me."

That sounds…exciting. I think about how it felt when he had his hands between my thighs, all oiled up and slick, and I squirm on the pillow. I press my legs together and focus on his thick shaft in front of me. The head of him bobs tantalizingly close to my face and I feel the insane urge to kiss it again. I stroke my fingers over him, petting and learning the feel of him. His cock is impossibly thick, the head tapered and protruding from the darker foreskin that sleeves it. As I stroke my fingers lightly over him again, the foreskin retreats back a little more, his cock seemingly harder and longer than before.

A droplet, barely visible in the darkness, beads on the tip.

I lick my lips again and glance up at him. "Can I taste you?"

"Oh, Iolanthe," he murmurs, and his thumb traces my lower lip. "I would love that."

I lean forward and lick the tip of him again. This time I'm anticipating the strong taste of him, and I don't pull back when the flavor hits my tongue. I lap up the salty drop, and his breath hitches. Another one appears, so I do it again, and then I keep my tongue there, swirling it around the head because he seems to like that. I glance up at him as I do, and his eyes are so dark in the shadows, his mouth parted. He should be utterly terrifying, but instead, I'm oddly thrilled. I love that he can't look away from me. I love that he keeps stroking my cheek and the legs I lean against feel tense. I love that his entire focus is on me and my mouth. I've never felt so alive as I do in this moment, so in control.

Lightly, I drag my teeth over the head of him.

He sucks in a breath. "You're going to be the death of me, Iolanthe."

"I want you alive," I whisper, and lick the spot I scraped. "I don't know how to pleasure you, though. I have no experience in this. Will you show me what you like?"

Agakor groans again, the sound pained. "How are you so sweet? Your father put far too small a price on your lovely head, my wife-to-be. You are a prize beyond riches." He takes one of my fluttering, stroking hands and cups it in his, guiding it onto his shaft until my palm is pressed against him. Then, he guides my fingers to curl around his length. He takes my hand and drags it up and down his length, the foreskin moving with my hand and making my fist glide up and down his shaft.

Oh. He likes it rougher then, harder. Understanding, I take

over and pump him eagerly with my hand, and when his grip relaxes on me, I know I'm doing it just as he likes. I lean in and press another kiss to the tip of his cock, just because I want to keep putting my mouth on him, and when he makes a sound of pleasure, I get bolder. I take the head of him between my lips and suck, thinking about how he'd put his mouth all over the sensitive bead of flesh between my thighs.

His breath hitches and his hand goes to my hair. "Gods. Gods, Iolanthe. That sweet little tongue of yours is wondrous."

He likes my tongue? I use it even more, teasing the head of his cock with little swirls before I suck him into my mouth again. He's too big for me to do more than tease the tip, but he doesn't seem to mind. It's as if Agakor likes my frantic, jerking hands and my hungry mouth on his cock. He murmurs encouragement as I stroke him, his gripping hand tightening in my hair as his hips twitch. Oh, that's a good sign. I work him frantically with my mouth, squeezing and pumping my fist, because I want him to have the same release I did.

"Move back," he breathes, the sound so muffled and strained that I don't hear it at first. He repeats it again, tugging gently on my hair this time. "Move back, Iolanthe. Now."

Quivering, I recoil. "Did I do something wrong—"

Before I can finish, he grips my hand again, using me to work his shaft. As he does, he throws his head back and I'm struck dumb at how rugged, how tortured, how handsome his primal face is. He's lost in the moment, his teeth bared, showing a pair of small upper fangs that match his much larger lower ones. It takes me a moment to realize that he's coming, and then I see a spurt of something into the air. It splatters on his bared thighs, and over my fist, which is still covered by his hand.

His cock erupts, overflowing with creamy ropes of what must be his seed, and I'm gasping in shock at the heat of him as he pours over my fingers.

"You," he finally manages with a ragged breath, his face strained, "were magnificent. I just didn't want to come in your mouth and frighten you the first time. Wanted you to see what you were getting into."

Oh. He was going to come into my mouth? With all that? I blink, astonished, because there's a lot of seed coating my hand and his thighs. A great, great deal. Curious, I lift my hand from his and lick a dripping fingertip, and I love the fierce groan he makes as he catches my actions.

It's still not my favorite taste, but oh, I like his response. I like it so much that I lick my fingers again, and I find the taste growing on me. "I thought I'd done something wrong," I confess, feeling sheepish. "You'd tell me if I did?"

"I told you you were perfect and I meant it," Agakor says. He grabs another cushion from the window seat and mops at my hand and his thighs, and I'm mutely horrified at the smears he's leaving on the poor cushion. "What?" he asks, when he catches my expression.

"I'm going to have to ask Turnip to clean that," I stammer. "Won't she know what we're up to?"

He chuckles, and the sound curls pleasantly in my belly. "You think she doesn't know already?"

Oh. *Oh.* "She does?"

"Aye, and if she's smart, she'll keep her mouth shut." He finishes mopping the worst of it with the poor ruffled pillow, and I use the hem of my innermost chemise to awkwardly help out. Once his thighs and our hands are no longer sticky, he hauls me into his arms and nuzzles at my neck, and I can feel the heat of his bare length pressing against my skirts. "My lovely, hungry bride," he murmurs, and he sounds thrilled. "I love your touch."

"I love touching you," I admit shyly. I reach up and caress his face, angling mine in the hopes of another kiss. "Can I do that again soon? I want to learn to do it perfectly."

Chuckling, Agakor runs his hands over me, pressing kisses to my neck. His tusks rub against my skin but I like it. I like all of him, honestly. He's different, but he makes me feel protected and safe, and his personality is so warm and generous that I forget that I'm supposed to be upset over marrying a half-orc. I forget that I'm supposed to find him ugly and unpleasant. There's nothing unpleasant about him in the slightest. "We'll save more rounds for after we're married," he promises me, his voice smooth and rich and delicious. One hand skims up my skirts, and then he's touching my thigh. "Wouldn't you rather have your turn now instead?"

I squirm a little at that, because I loved his mouth on me. It felt so good, so raw and open and shameless. At the same time, I still feel shy. It's odd to ask for something like that. *Yes, can you please tongue me between my legs until I fall apart?* I want to be as bold as him, but it seems when I'm asking for myself, it's far more difficult. The words lock in my throat and I end up pressing my face against his neck, embarrassed.

"Too much for you?" he murmurs, cradling me against him. "You are yet shy, love? You begged to tongue my cock but cannot ask for your own pleasure?"

"'S different," I mumble against his throat. He's warm and masculine-smelling right here, and I want to stay just like this forever. "I was always told a lady's job is to please her husband."

"Ahhh." His thumb rubs against the inside of my thigh, under my skirts. "But no one tells ladies they should demand anything for themselves, mm?" At my wordless nod, his hand slides between my legs. "Then you can just tell me quietly… should I stop?"

I shake my head, my nose pressed against his neck. "Don't stop," I manage to whisper, even though my face is burning with embarrassment. "Please."

"Nothing you ask me for is embarrassing," Agakor tells me, voice achingly low and rumbly. He teases little circles on the insides of my thighs, making me twitch and driving me wild with yearning. "We are to be husband and wife. If you came to me every day and asked me to lick your pretty cunt until you came, I would gladly do so. Not only is it my duty as your husband, but it is a *pleasure.*"

I whimper.

His fingers skim up to my folds, and when one thick digit parts them, moving slowly up and down, I can scarcely breathe. "Look at how wet you are for me now," he murmurs. "You like my cock. You like my touch. I like how honeyed this cunt is. It's going to be such a good marriage, my sweet."

Biting back a moan, I fist my hands into his tunic as he finds the bead at the apex of my folds and begins to tease it with one blunt fingertip. I rock against his touch, working myself against his hand and muffling my noises of pleasure against his throat. Just like last night, the tickling ache builds up to a hot yearning and then something more, something that grows and grows, building toward urgency, until my body is making obscenely wet sounds as he works my cunt with wet, practiced fingers, whispering naughty, filthy things in my ears about what he wants to do to me.

When I come, my body curls up and I bend over around his hand, clasping it tight between my thighs. Even then, he teases my clit with a stroking finger, until I'm falling apart and gasping on his lap, the insides of my thighs soaked and my body exhausted from my release. I slump against him, sighing heavily, and manage a smile when he presses kiss after kiss to my cheek.

"My lovely, lusty little maiden," he says, pleased. "I need the full moon to get here quickly."

"Two days," I agree. "Like your father said."

"Forever," he grumbles.

It does feel like forever. Smiling, I lean up and give him a happy kiss on the jaw. "After that, we're done, right?"

"Gods, I hope so."

Agakor

Two days, I tell myself. I can last two more days. Two more days and then I'll fall upon my sweet human bride and rut until the dawn. Two days and then she'll be officially mine…well, once the orc ceremony of mating is complete. I'm not looking forward to that part. My father is thrilled, of course. He doesn't care that I take a human bride, but he wants her to be fierce, like my mother was. Iolanthe is many things, but she is definitely not my father's idea of fierce. But she is smart and eager and loyal, and she pleases me.

Greatly.

So it does not matter what my father wants. I ignore his

teasing, just as I ignore the teasing of the rest of the Redbloom Clan. They are my father's clan, not mine. They can think what they like, as long as they don't upset Iolanthe. So I watch her carefully for the next two days. I don't head out to survey my lands, even though word keeps trickling in that Lord Purnav of Rockmourn is rallying his forces. I stay at the keep and I make sure that everyone is treating my bride properly, because the thought of someone being cruel to Iolanthe is like a knife to the gut.

How could anyone be cruel to someone so achingly sweet? But my men are rough and ready. They are not used to being around ladies and are far more at home with my father's wild orc band than around gently reared Iolanthe. Perhaps that's why I feel so protective of her. Skirmishes, I know how to handle. Battle, I am familiar with.

But the thought of someone being cruel to my perfect, pretty bride destroys me. It leaves me helpless. So I hover around the keep and try not to make it look as if I'm worried. My father knows me well, though, and just smirks every time he catches me stealing a glance towards her. He knows what a big deal it is for an orc—even a half-orc—to marry a fine lady. When I imagined myself taking a human lady as a bride, I didn't think further than that. I wanted a son to cement my claim upon this land, and a bride to ensure that I would look legitimate in the eyes of the other lords. I want them to see me as just another lord, not a squatter or an interloper who bought his way to a lord's title and keep with coin. A bride was just another piece of the puzzle, another way to get respect. I imagined her as something to endure, someone that would be horrified at who she had to marry, but who would put up with me because of the gold I paid her father.

I never imagined someone like Iolanthe. Someone who would shyly meet me in all my desires, someone who is as fascinated at touching me as I am with her. Someone who looks at my run-down keep as her home and even now works to clean it from top to bottom and make it presentable. I didn't imagine that my wife would like me, much less be eager for my touch.

From the moment she petted my cock like it was a puppy, she's held my heart in her hand.

I can do two days, I tell myself. If Iolanthe is brave enough to go through all these demanding wedding ceremonies with me, I can manage to wait two more days.

The evening of the full moon is clear and cold. My keep is brimming with my father's men and my own. More rumors swirl around Lord Purnav, but I'm prepared for whatever comes next. If he thinks to rob me, he's in for a surprise. My men might be uncouth, but they're brutal warriors and loyal to me. If he thinks to steal Iolanthe back and demand a ransom, his head is going to end up on a pike at my gates.

No one's touching my bride but me.

There's no feast this night, and I wear my hunting leathers as I strap weapons to my chest and put on heavy boots. I tie my hair back in the traditional knot high atop my head, just as my father wears his.

Mudag asks, "Will you wear flowers in your hair? Show honor to your father's clan?"

I roll my eyes at him as I sheathe a knife at my belt and tie a pouch full of rations next to it. "Father, I'm honoring you with this ceremony. Your flowers are choking me."

"Of course they're strong. It hides your scent." He lifts his chin, arrogant. "That's the purpose."

"I don't need to hide my scent," I point out, brushing a bit of lint off my tunic. "Iolanthe has a human nose. She won't even hear me coming, much less smell me." I pause, and then add, "Unless I wear the flowers. Then she'll smell me from a league away."

"Bah. She's no woman like your mother." He crosses his arms over his chest. "I doubt she will lead you on a very merry chase."

I don't care if she stops three paces ahead of me and gives up. "I'm still marrying her."

Mudag grunts.

I try not to roll my eyes at my father's surliness and head back inside the keep, searching for my bride. We're to ride out to the woods at the edge of my estate and perform our "mating ceremony" there, since the land around my stronghold is nothing but rolling plains and scattered farms. Iolanthe told me she'd wear something practical, but I'm not entirely sure she owns anything that isn't ruffled and covered in a dozen layers of skirts. She needs practical gear for tonight. An orc mating is basically a chase, hunter and prey. I don't want her wearing some ridiculous gown that's going to get shredded the moment I find her.

Because once an orc catches his prey, he claims her. Well, traditionally.

There are more traditions at stake here than just mine, though, and Iolanthe is being a good sport about all of this. I'm not going to make our first mating on the forest floor. I'll chase her down, tap her lightly with the club, and then we'll find someplace safe to bunk. The next morning, I'll allow her to escape me and head back to the keep with the horse I'll be keeping nearby for her, and when she returns, we'll have the final ceremony. It's just a lot of posturing to please my father and his clan.

Even so, I'm more pleased than I thought I'd be that she's willing to do this with me.

I head through the keep, looking for my bride. The servants are scraping old drips of wax from the walls, and the place smells fresh and clean. Day by day, it's becoming more of a home under Iolanthe's command, and I love that. I don't see my bride or her ancient chaperone anywhere, so I head upstairs to the solar. When she's not there, I try the bedroom. "Iolanthe?"

My bride immediately opens the door, beaming at me. She's dressed entirely in deep red, in full skirts with an embroidered bodice that pushes her tits up magnificently. A tiny decorative chain across the front panel of her bodice emphasizes the heave of her breasts, and her sleeves are puffy and full, decorated with ribbons. Those ribbons match the artful loops that lace together the heavy panels of her skirts in a peekaboo fashion that give tantalizing glimpses of the chemise underneath. She's beautiful, of course.

It's also completely the wrong thing to wear for the occasion. I shake my head at her. "You'll have to change."

Iolanthe chews on her lower lip, glancing down at her dress. "This is my oldest gown. I didn't bring very many with me, Agakor, and we've already torn one."

Right, for the first night's ceremony. I stare at her clothing. Now that she mentions it, the plush red of her dress is faded in certain spots, and the artful ribbons are frayed. The enticing chain across her tits is tarnished, but there's no denying she's still far too overdressed for me to chase her down in the woods. "How many dresses do you have total?" I ask.

Her cheeks grow pink and she ducks her head, tugging on her bodice like she does when she's anxious. I've noticed that small movement of hers. "Four. Well, three now. But I can mix and match the pieces—"

Exasperated, I stare at her gown. A new idea hits me and I grab her by the hand. "Come with me."

Iolanthe

Hours later, I'm seated atop one of the horses in a completely inappropriate outfit and trying not to squirm. I've never, ever worn pants before. They fit odd. My legs feel loose, and I actually miss the swish and heavy comfort of my skirts against my legs. The only thing I like about this is that I'm wearing one of Agakor's warm tunics, and an old belt of his is cinched at my waist, along with a dagger. The cloak I wear is dark and heavy, but it smells like him and it's warm.

I'm not sure how I let him talk me into wearing men's clothes, but I'm not a fan of it. I want my dresses back, even though I understand they're not appropriate for tonight's ceremony. I just feel oddly naked without a bodice to keep everything in place, or the heavy rustle of the chemise against my legs. It's just adding to my unease about tonight's ceremony.

It's not that I'm worried about "marrying" Agakor in the traditional orc way. It's that it entails me racing off through the dark woods under the full moon. I'm not an outdoorsy woman. I like being home with my books and my sewing. I like cozy nights by the fire and having a clean house. I don't like hunting, or riding, and I sure don't like pants.

But I like Agakor, and I want him to be proud of me, so here I am. He rides at my side on the biggest horse I've ever seen, and his men are not far behind. A few orcs race behind the horses, chaperones for tonight's ceremony. I'm told that they'll be in the woods, scent-tracking what happens with us but not actually viewing anything so they can give us "privacy."

It makes me wonder if brides in the past were claimed in the dirt, if their new husbands kissed them everywhere in the darkness and made them their wives under the trees. I don't know if I find that appalling or completely and utterly titillating. Agakor promised this won't happen for us, and I suppose that's a good thing.

I…suppose.

Agakor draws up, his massive horse prancing. "This is as good a place as any."

It is? I eye my surroundings. It's very dark outside, the moon bright and blood red in the skies overhead. Stars cover the sky, but they're not providing enough light as far as I'm concerned. Everything is in shadow—the stream we crossed a few minutes ago, the thick forest ahead of us, the big half-orc at my side. Even my horse looks slightly ominous in the darkness. I reach out and pat her neck, reassuring myself that she's fine and we're all safe.

My husband-to-be dismounts, and several of the other men do as well. Before I can slide off my horse, Agakor is at my side, helping me dismount, and I'm filled with another affectionate rush of emotion for him. I can get down off a horse on my own, of course, but it's nice that he's hovering over me as if I'm precious and dainty. Flustered, I notice that his hands linger at my waist and he takes more than one look at my legs, outlined as they are in the obscene pants. The rest of the orc runners splash across the stream, joining us, and I pull the cloak tighter around me as we wait for the others to settle in and get ready for the ceremony. My breath puffs in the air in front of me, but I'm not cold as much as I am nervous.

Really, really nervous.

Mudag strolls up to us. Tendrils of his hair float on the night breeze, and in the shadows, Agakor looks just like him. He puts a hand on Agakor's shoulder, his dark eyes shining with pride. "My son. Today, you will catch yourself a bride. As your father and leader of Redbloom Clan, I could not be more proud."

Behind us, the orcs stomp their feet with approval, whistling and calling out Agakor's name.

Mudag raises an arm in the air, brandishing a club aloft. I blanch at the sight of a spike tipping the end of it, and what looks like chain wrapped around the thick part at the end. "This is the club my father gave me when I chose a bride, and it is the club I shall give you so you may choose yours." He lowers it and holds it out to Agakor. "Use it well, my son."

I'm alarmed at how misty-eyed Agakor looks as Mudag

hands him the horrid-looking weapon. "Thank you, my father. I will honor you and the clan with its use."

One of the orcs at the edge of the group starts to sing a song. I don't understand the words, as they're called out in an orkish tongue. But the song grows with excitement and intensity as others join in, singing and clapping, the words speeding up as Agakor turns to look at me.

I give another wary look to the club in his hands.

"Ceremonial," he whispers. "I promise."

I swallow hard. Do I trust him? I think of how he's been around me and decide that yes, I do. I agreed to the custom of the orc wedding. I trust Agakor not to hurt me. Not when he's kissed me so tenderly and touched me in ways that make me ache all over. He doesn't want me dead. He wants me alive and willing and in his bed. So I straighten proudly and look up at him.

"You have five minutes," he announces to me when the song ends.

"Five minutes for what?"

"To run," Agakor tells me. His black eyes gleam in the moonlight. "And then I am going to chase you."

A hot, terrified little thrill shoots through me. "What's going to happen when you catch me?"

The look on his face turns wicked. "Everything."

I turn and race into the woods.

Breathless, I scramble through the dark woods. I stumble over dead branches and plants tear at the cloak I wear, but I can't stop running. There's an odd, erotic excitement to the fact that I'm being chased through the forest on the night of a full moon. Even more thrilling is knowing what happens when Agakor "catches" me. I'm sure he'll do more than just kiss me once and send me on my way. Last night, we'd met in the solar again and I'd ridden his hand until I came, and bit a hole into the sleeve of his tunic with my teeth. I imagine him chasing after me, tackling me to the ground…and then licking me between my thighs until I'm wild with lust, and I'm so aroused I can't think straight.

I run fast. I know the goal is for him to catch me, but I still want to make him work for it. I want the orcs of his father's tribe to be proud of the chase I take Agakor on. So I run as fast as I can, stumbling my way through the undergrowth. I slide down a muddy bank and into a creek, only to catch myself and get back on my feet, racing forward once more. Even though I'm a lady, I'm strong. I'm on my feet all day at home, helping run the keep, and I can take big steps to eat up the ground.

I'm going to have to be fast, because he's going to be able to find me on my scent alone. Just the thought makes another hot prickle move through me, and my breath sobs into the air. *Faster*, I warn myself as I catch my breath, leaning against a tree. *Run faster.*

I picture the enormous club with the spike on the end, and

that gets my feet moving.

Dashing through the trees, I skid to a halt when I come upon the edge of a cliff. I halt and take a few steps forward, peering over to see how far below the ground is. It's not too far, maybe three times my height. Below me, it looks as if half the hill has crumbled away into rock, with a few branches hanging over the sides. Since I can't go straight, I follow along the edge of the cliff, looking for a way down.

As I do, I hear a man's laugh.

I draw up short, worried that Agakor has found me already. Hot excitement pulses through me, and I look around for the next spot to dash to. There's a cluster of trees up ahead, and I race off once more, heading for their protection in the hopes that it'll slow down my soon-to-be husband.

Being chased is *so* thrilling. I thought it was silly at first, but now that he's hunting me, I don't think I've ever been more aroused. I both want him to catch me and I'm terrified of (and excited about) what happens when he does. I hear a twig snap behind me, and I lunge forward through the trees—

—an arm snags around my waist.

I squeal, loud and breathless. He's caught me! Anticipation flares, but when a strong hand grabs my jaw and forces my head back, my excited senses change to flat terror. The arm around my waist is cruel, and the hand that clutches my face is bruisingly tight. I stare into the eyes of one of my father's most trusted knights.

"By all the gods," he breathes, just as shocked to see me. "It's Lady Iolanthe."

Another man emerges from the shadows a few steps behind him. They're both dressed in dark colors, hoods pulled over their heads. Immediately, I realize what this is. My father has sent out scouts. They're lurking in these woods—Agakor's woods—and are going to attack my husband or his men. I have to do something, and quick.

As both men stare at me, I realize the second is clutching a knife. Both of them are wearing swords, and there are dark smears on their faces, as if trying to disguise their pale skin at night. An ambush. That's what this is. So I use a woman's best defense—tears. I immediately burst into sobs. "You've saved me!"

They're clearly taken aback by my theatrics. The tight, bruising hands on me loosen and fall away. "Lady—"

I fling myself against my captor, like the terrified woman I'm supposed to be. "You're taking me home with you, aren't you? Please say you are! My father's sent you to rescue me, has he not?" I weep loudly and balefully, all the while my mind frantically working. "Surely that's why you're here?"

"Ah, lady..." The closest one pats me on the shoulder. "Your father was planning on rescuing you soon, never fear."

"But not tonight?" I wail.

They give each other alarmed looks, and one puts a finger to his lips. "Please, quiet, if you will, Lady Iolanthe. These woods are surrounded by orcs."

Of course they are. I rode out here with them. But I pretend to sniffle and be a weak, simpering fool. "Then you've saved me."

The men exchange a look again. "We're scouting," blurts the second. "We have a mission to complete—"

"No mission is more important than returning me to my father's side, don't you agree?" I cling to the first man's tunic, an unhinged and slightly desperate look on my face. "Father will be glad if you take me home first!"

They're silent. I realize, to my dawning horror, that this isn't part of the plan at all. My father isn't sending these men to rescue me. They're not here scouting on innocent things. They're here to gather information and report back to my father. All at once, I see why they're so reluctant at the sight of me. My father can't protest and demand my return if I've already returned. He can't demand me back safely if I'm home. He can't pick a fight and sack Agakor's keep if there's no reason to attack.

I thought Agakor was wrong, that my father would never mount an army to retrieve me. Well, I was half right. He's mounting an army, but it's not to retrieve me. It's to rob Agakor under the pretense of rescuing me. It's obvious by the way these men act, as if I'm a problem they must suddenly solve.

"How did you get out here, Lady Iolanthe?" the second, more skeptical one asks.

I lower my voice, pretending to be terrified. Actually, I'm not pretending. Somewhere out in these dark woods is my sweet Agakor. If these men find him, they're going to attack him. There could be more of my father's men out here, too. He's in danger, and I have to somehow fix this. "They're hunting me," I mock-whisper. "It's an orkish wedding tradition. He's going to find me and club me over the head. Why do you think I'm so panicked?"

Their eyes widen and they exchange another look. "I wish we could bring you with us, Lady Iolanthe," one begins, regret clear in his tone. "It's just…we have a mission…"

"Please," I weep, trying to be as pitiful as possible. I fall to the ground, letting the cloak settle around me. As it does, I feel along the dirt, searching for something to use as a weapon. I need a fist-sized rock, or something with heft. When my searching fingers clamp around a branch, as thick as my wrist, I slide it under my cloak and get to my feet again. "Please, you can't leave me here."

"My lady…"

There's a crash in the bushes nearby, and both men immediately turn away from me, their gazes locked on the dark woods. One draws his sword and takes a step forward.

I raise the branch high above my head and slam it down on the back of his skull as hard as I can. The crack is enormous, and the branch splinters in my grip. A split second later, Agakor emerges from the woods and clubs the other man over the head.

When they're both at our feet, he looks at me, panting. The half-orc is gorgeous in the pale moonlight, deadly and protective all at once. "Did they hurt you, Iolanthe? Tell me and I'll snap their necks."

I manage to shake my head. "I'm okay," I breathe. And then I point at the man collapsed at his feet. "But I think you just married that one."

He stares at me for a long moment. Then, he breaks into laughter, and it's the sweetest sound I've ever heard.

Agakor

I've never felt so frightened in my life as I was in those moments Iolanthe was with her father's soldiers.

At first, I was terrified for her life. I'd been not far behind her, and when the one soldier caught her around the waist and she screamed, I swear I aged twenty years in that moment. It took everything I had not to attack. I couldn't be certain that they wouldn't hurt her or use her as a shield against me. I needed to think. I needed to keep the advantage of the shadows.

And then, Iolanthe had started to cry and beg them to take her back to her father. She'd cried so earnestly and so pitifully that a new ache overtook me. Was this real? Had she been pretending all along to be eager to marry me? The thought made my heart feel as if it was made of ash. To think that all those moments we'd stolen together, her eager kisses, her sweet laughter, as all lies...

But then she clubbed one of the men over the head, and I felt like I could breathe again.

A short time later, I have both men bound and gagged. I grab each one by a fistful of his clothing and drag him behind me as Iolanthe trots at my side, a worried expression on her pretty face as we head back to my father's men. I'm angry. Angry that these fools are on my land. Angry that Iolanthe's father is such a woale-turd of a man.

Angry that yet another wedding ceremony has been interrupted. Do the gods hate me? Am I never going to claim Iolanthe as mine? My balls are going to permanently ache at this rate.

Mudag isn't surprised when I show up with the two soldiers in tow. I toss them at his feet, disgusted at how this night is going. "We need information from them. What they're doing on my land, what Lord Purnav's plans are. What they plan for my bride."

My father grunts, hands on hips. He lifts his chin, looking at me and Iolanthe. "You finish your capture-games?"

"No," I say, annoyed. I was busy protecting my bride-to-be.

"Night's half over," he tells me, looking over at Iolanthe. "She doesn't look like she's been clubbed."

"I have not been," my helpful bride agrees. She dusts off her clothes and tosses her hair back. "Should we get going, then, Agakor?"

Not much takes me by surprise, but this female does. I gape

at her for a moment. "You…you want to continue?"

Iolanthe's brows furrow. "This has to be done on a full moon, does it not?" She points up at the sky hidden behind the trees. "Full moon. We're already out here. Might as well keep going."

I shake my head. "I don't like this. Those men grabbed you. What if the next one decides to take you back to your father? There could be more of them combing the woods. There could be an entire band of mercenaries just waiting on the edge of the forest. It's safer to go back home."

Iolanthe tilts her head at me, and then the stubborn woman shakes her head. "No. We're doing it tonight. I'm not waiting another month to marry you."

"But those soldiers—"

"You'll just have to catch me quickly," she says, and darts back into the woods before I can protest more.

My father laughs, the sound hearty and amused. "Reminds me of your mother, that one. Never could win an argument with her." He slaps me on the back affectionately. "Better go catch your bride, son. Club her good."

Club her. More like I want to grab her and shake her for being so headstrong. With a sigh, I set off into the woods after her. I drag my feet at first, wanting to give her a sporting chance of getting away from me. Then I remember that the woods are dangerous, and I speed up. Iolanthe's light scent is all over the nighttime forest, and to my relief, it's the only one I'm picking up. That doesn't mean others aren't in the vicinity. They could be upwind. I just need to remain on guard…and I need to catch my mate.

I wait a brief time, letting her race ahead of me and putting distance between us and the orc party at the edge of the woods.

When I decide that things have gone on far enough, I speed up, sneaking behind Iolanthe. She's crashing through the forest, noisy enough to wake the dead, and I decide that's enough of that. Moving to Iolanthe's side, I surge forward and snatch her into my embrace. She makes the most charming squeal, flinging her arms around my neck and holding on as I continue to run.

"Where are we going?" she protests as I carry her through the forest. "You caught me!"

"We're finding a cave. And then we're going to hide out for the rest of the night so everyone knows I've captured you." Luckily, I know just the spot. There's a small cave not far from here, and I've stayed there overnight in the past when a storm caught me while out hunting. It's hidden enough that I don't think Lord Purnav's men would have found it. If they have, I'll just crack their heads and drag them back to my father again, I suppose.

But we're finishing this ceremony tonight. I won't put her in danger again. I already hate that we're back out here in the woods, because every protective instinct I have is telling me to turn around and take her back to my keep. To lock every door behind her and set a dozen guards in front of each one. To wrap her in blankets and make sure no one can get to her. I don't care about the coin that her father is after (though it does irk me that he thinks he can steal from me). I care about her. Iolanthe's safety is everything.

She doesn't protest the idea of a cave, though. She just clings to me as I move through the underbrush, as silently as possible. We run into no one else, and I feel a little better about having my bride-to-be out here in the woods with me. I find the entrance of the cave—a narrow, craggy crack in the middle of a rocky bluff—and squeeze my way inside. Iolanthe winces at the sound of my tunic tearing on a sharp edge, burying her face against my chest. "Agakor! Are you okay?"

"It's just my tunic," I reassure her. "I'm fine." Luckily the cave opens up a bit farther away from the mouth, so I have room to stretch out. I gently set her on her feet and run my hands all over her arms and legs. I'm pretty sure she's all right, but a branch could have sliced at her soft skin while I ran, or she could have been pricked by thorns. "You're all right, too, yes? You'd tell me if you weren't?"

"I'm perfectly fine." She smiles up at me in the darkness, and I can tell by the way her eyes search for my face that she can't see me. "And you? Are you all right?"

"I will be. I'm going to do a quick scouting run to make sure no one is nearby." I pull the club out of its holster over my shoulder. "You take this and you club anyone that comes in here, all right?"

"But then will I have to marry them?" Iolanthe jokes, a nervous wobble in her voice.

I cup her face and give her a quick, fierce kiss. "You're not marrying anyone but me, woman." I'm pleased when she chuckles. It makes me feel momentarily better about having to leave her alone for a short time. "I promise I'll return quickly."

"Okay," she whispers, and then holds the club, waiting as she stares at the entrance. "I'll be here."

Filled with pride, I gaze at my bride-to-be. She's taken this all in stride, from strange marriage customs to this attack tonight. Nothing fazes her gentle, resilient nature, not even that she's about to marry a half-orc. Truly, the gods are looking down on our union...provided we ever get to the altar and complete the act. But first, safety. I slip back out of the cave, further shredding my tunic, and head back into the trees. A short time later, I'm comfortable that there's no one nearby. All the scents in the forest are old except ours. I circle back toward the cave, giving Iolanthe a warning as I step back inside. "All clear."

With a sigh of relief, she holds the club back out to me. "This is yours, then."

I take it from her, leaning it against the wall. "I have no plans on using it on you. My father will know by our twined scents that I found you and we're spending tonight together."

"I didn't think you were really going to club me," she admits, reaching out in the darkness. When her hands find my tunic, she moves closer and pulls me into a hug. "I was worried when I ran into the soldiers, though."

I stroke her hair, loving the feel of her smaller body pressed against mine. "I was, too. I heard you crying and begging them to take you back, and I thought it was the truth. I thought all this time you were pretending that you wanted to be with me, all so your father could keep my coins." At her choked gasp, I take her by the shoulders. "You do know that you don't have to marry me, right? If this isn't what you want, I understand. I'll take you back to your father's doorstep, no questions asked. I promise I want what makes you happy."

She's silent, and my chest aches with the realization that she's considering things. Of course she is. Marrying a half-orc isn't anyone's dream of a husband. I have a keep and I'm wealthy, but no title to go with it. Likely she was imagining herself in an entirely different scenario and the reality of it is disappointing. It hurts me, but I want her happiness. When I originally approached her father about seeking a bride, I didn't concern myself with her feelings. To me, that wasn't important. But now that I know Iolanthe better and I know what a prize she is, all I can think about is that she needs the best the world can offer.

And it's not me.

"Iolanthe," I begin, determined to pick the right course of action.

She silences me by putting her hand on my cock. "I think you should ruin me, Agakor. Tonight."

Iolanthe

Agakor is silent. I wonder if I've done something wrong, or perhaps offended him by grabbing his length.

"You…don't want me to take you back to your father?" His tone is confused. I can't see his face in the darkness of the cave. "I thought that was what you'd want."

Is he serious? How could he possibly think that? I rub my hand up and down his length, and it stiffens under my touch immediately. That's both gratifying and exciting. I like that I can make him so excited with just a touch. And he thinks I want to return to my father? To a life of being utterly forgotten? "You seriously don't mean that."

"I want you to be happy, Iolanthe. I'm not cultured. I'm not even fully human."

I give his cock a squeeze to silence him. "I'm marrying you and that's final. I don't like that my father is doing this. I hate it. I hate that he's lied to both of us about everything." I rub the bulge in his pants. "I think you should take my virginity. Tonight. Ruin me so no one can stop a marriage between us from going through."

He chokes for a moment. "You…you can't be serious."

"I'm very serious." I slide my other arm around his waist, pressing myself against him even as I stroke that enticing length. "I don't have much of a reputation to lose. My father is a noble with an old title, but little money. Everyone already thinks we're to be married. What's the harm in taking me now? If you claim me, my father won't be able to take me from you." I outline his cock with my fingers in lazy strokes. "Don't you want me?"

Agakor's breathing rasps heavily in my ear. He squeezes my shoulders. Once. Twice. "Iolanthe. You know I want you."

"I want you, too."

"Your first time shouldn't be in a cave."

"I don't care where my first time is, as long as it's with you," I confess. "I just want to be yours. How many marriage ceremonies must we have before you'll finally make me yours?"

With a low growl, he fists his hand in my tangled hair and tilts my head back. A moment later, his mouth crashes down on mine. I bite back a gasp of pleased surprise, opening up to receive his kiss. Our mouths don't fit together perfectly—his is too wide and his tusks get in the way, but it doesn't matter. I love the passion, the dip of his tongue against mine, the way that he moves his lips against my face. I love all of it and I want so much more. "You want to be mine?" he asks, voice ragged. "Tonight?"

"More than anything."

I smile into the darkness. "Then touch me."

He kisses me again, his mouth gentle on mine. Then he kisses down my neck, nuzzling and licking at the sensitive skin of my throat. "You deserve a big bed and soft blankets," he murmurs between kisses. "A fire to keep you warm. Wine to keep your thirst away. Candlelight—"

I grab at his topknot and tug on it. "I want this now," I remind him. "I don't care that this is a cave or that it's cold out. I just want to be yours. No more waiting, Agakor."

"No more waiting," he agrees, and then his hand is at the belt at my waist. He tugs it loose, letting it fall to the floor. "Can I undress you?"

"I wish you would."

Agakor chuckles. "You are so eager, no matter what I throw at you." He tugs at the hem of my borrowed tunic, hauling it upward. "How did I get so lucky?"

"You gave my father a wagonful of gold?" I tease. "Is that luck?" I shiver in the cold as he pulls the tunic over my head and I'm left topless. I'm much more familiar with having a chemise to cover my bare skin, and I cross my arms over my chest. My breasts are large and not especially perky, and it feels better when they're confined in a tight bodice that hauls everything into its correct place. Having everything hang loose is…awkward. At least it's dark.

But then Agakor tugs my hand away. "Let me look at you."

"You can see in this?" I hold a hand out, wiggling my fingers, and I can't even see it in front of me.

"I can. Orcs have excellent vision." He pulls my hands away and when I let them drop to my sides, I hear his breath hiss. "Look at you. So damned beautiful."

My skin prickles and my nipples tighten at his response. It takes everything I have to remain still and not cover myself again, because he wants to gaze upon me. I want him to look, too. I want him to be pleased with everything about me, just like I am with him. I don't even care that he's a half-orc or that his father likes to wear garlands of flowers to disguise his scent. I just enjoy being with Agakor. I love the way he makes me feel. I love how protective he is and that he makes me laugh.

And I really, really love his touch.

I gasp when a big, warm hand palms my breast. A moment later, he covers me with his other hand, and then he toys with both of them. "Gods, Iolanthe. I didn't think there would be anything better than your freckles, but your freckles on these beauties takes my breath away."

He likes my freckles? I want to ask about that, but his thumbs move over my nipples and then everything in my head goes blank. Dazed, I stand still as he teases them into points, and heat pulses through me. Him teasing the tips of my breasts makes me almost as heated as when his fingers are between my thighs. He's never touched my breasts until now, and I had no idea it could feel so very nice.

"Say something," Agakor murmurs. "Is this all right?"

"It feels good," I manage, shivering when his thumb strokes over one tight nipple. "You've never touched them before."

"You usually have them cinched up to your chin in one of your dresses," he agrees. I hear a shifting of fabric, and then a moment later, a hot, hungry mouth clasps over one nipple. I cry out as he groans his pleasure. "And you taste just as sweet as I imagined."

"Agakor," I pant. "Oh, gods."

"Such pretty breasts," he murmurs against my skin. His tusks graze my sensitive flesh as he teases the tip of one breast and then moves to the other. When my fluttering, helpless hands land on his hair, I realize he's dropped to his knees in front of me, and I sink my fingers into the knot of hair atop his skull. It feels good to have something to hold onto as he loops one big arm around my waist and hauls me in, his mouth latching on my breast. "Could tongue these beauties for hours."

Gasping, I squirm against him. I want that, but at the same time, I want him to fully claim me. I want his touch everywhere, and I'm feeling greedy. I slide a hand to his tunic and grab a fistful of it. "I want to feel you bare, too."

"Mmm, beg me for it," he says, and nips at the tip of my breast again.

With a moan, I stagger against him. My knees feel weak, hot need pulsing through me as he lavishes attention on my breasts. It's unfair how good his mouth feels, how everything inside me clenches when he sucks hard, his other hand working my neglected breast. "Please," I whisper. "Please let me feel you, too."

Tonguing little circles around my nipple until I whimper, he finally relents. "Just for you." I hear the rustle of his clothing, and then the light slap of fabric hitting the floor of the cave. Then his hands are on the waist of my pants. "A piece of clothing for a piece of clothing."

For some reason, that makes me laugh. Maybe because I'm

tingling all over from the kisses he gave my breasts, or maybe because it seems silly to try to compete on the number of pieces of clothing. "If you want me naked, just say so."

"I want you naked. I thought that was obvious."

I'm more comfortable, now, and there's so much need throbbing through me that I don't care about being nude. I kick off my boots and shimmy out of my pants, my toes curling on the cold cave floor. This time, they aren't fun goosebumps but those of a chill, and I rub my arms.

"Cold?" he asks, his hand stroking down my bare arm. "Come here, and I'll warm you up."

I take a step forward, and I'm immediately in the circle of his arms. He kisses me again, his hands moving over my bare skin, and when I press forward, I can feel the scorching length of him between us. Oh. I didn't realize he'd gotten undressed while I did. I can feel every bit of his naked skin, from his hard, hairy thighs to the hair covering his muscular abdomen. He's nothing like I daydreamed a husband would be. When I was a young girl, I imagined a sweet-faced knight with pale hair and pretty eyes, who would delicately hold my hand and read me poems.

The reality is so much better.

"How are we going to do this?" I whisper, stroking my hand over his cock again. I can't resist touching him. I love his reactions, love the heated feel of him in my grip. "Do I need to get on my hands and knees?"

Agakor cups my face and gives me another hungry kiss. "I'll sit on the floor and you can sit atop me."

I blink at that, because I can't picture how it could possibly work. It goes against everything I've ever seen one of my father's animals do. But I trust Agakor knows more about this than I do, and so I wait, shivering.

He describes his actions in the darkness to me—that he's putting his cloak down to sit on, that he's moving to the floor. Then he touches my hand and guides me forward, until I stand over him. I sink down, straddling his thighs, and his cock presses against the heated flesh between my thighs. I suck in a breath at how raw and urgent it feels, and his arms go around me again, hauling me closer and pulling me in for another kiss.

"This all right?" he asks between kisses.

I nod, breathless. "Feels good." And it does. My breasts are pushing against his big, solid chest. My feet are off of the cold floor, my knees on either side of him cradled on the cloak. His hands are all over me, warming me up, and I feel cherished and loved...and very, very aroused. "I just don't know what I'm supposed to do."

"Are you wet?" He holds my backside in his big hands and drags me forward against his shaft. I gasp as he rocks me against it, and the feel of his cock slipping through my folds is like nothing I've ever felt before. Dear goddess Belara, it's a lot. But when he kisses me again, I find that I rock back against his length once more. It feels so good to rub against him. It teases the hunger inside me, making me yearn for more. "Aye, you're wet," he murmurs. "I can feel you getting my cock all wet with your juices."

His lips play against mine, and I mewl, clinging to his neck as I kiss him frantically. "Aren't you supposed to be inside me?"

"Greedy wife," Agakor chuckles. "Don't you want me to make you come first?"

I shake my head. Normally I'd want that, but right now, I

just want him inside me, filling me up. I feel hollow, with a deep ache between my thighs that I've never felt before. "I just want you. Tonight. Now."

Agakor groans, and his mouth locks on mine, his tongue flicking playfully against my own. His hand slips between us as I rock against his cock, and I whimper when he presses a big finger to the entrance of my body. It feels enormous when he pushes deeper, my breath stuttering against his lips. "I need to stretch you or this isn't going to work, love. Do you trust me?"

I manage a nod, biting down on his lower lip. Our mouths keep moving over one another, even though we're not really kissing anymore. It's just frantic motions, one desperately tasting the other as he fingers me. I bite back a cry when he pushes deep inside me, because it feels like too much. Too much, and it's just a finger. I have no idea how we're going to do this, and a tendril of worry threads through my thoughts. "M-maybe we should have brought oil?"

He kisses me, mouth surprisingly soft against mine. "I've got you, love. It'll be fine. I promise. Just rock yourself on my hand. Make your body feel good, hmm?"

He thrusts deep into me, and I gasp against his lips, clinging to him. That felt like a lot, but when he thrusts again, it doesn't feel nearly as tight as it did. He pumps his finger into me a few more times, murmuring about what a good wife I am, and how sweet I feel on his hand, and then he adds a second finger, and the tightness starts all over again. I'm not sure I like this part, because it's uncomfortable and my body is making wet, sloppy sounds that are obscene in the darkness, but Agakor's mouth is sweet and reassuring on mine.

"Does that feel good?"

I hesitate a moment, wondering if I should lie. "It's different."

He chuckles, pressing more fervent kisses to me. "That's a no, then. I know what will help." He strokes his paired fingers deep into me again, and this time, his thumb grazes through my folds. He presses it against my clit and when he pumps into me again, it moves. This time, I whimper, and it's not with confusion. That feels good. Really good. And having his fingers inside me changes how everything feels. "That's better," he breathes. "That's my sweet wife."

Moaning, I rock on his hand as he continues to work two fingers deep into my body, his thumb teasing the button of my clit. This time, when he adds a third finger, I suck in a breath but it still feels all right. Tight, but the tightness quickly goes away from his encouraging words and the feel of his thumb on my clit, toying with me until I'm rocking frantically against his hand, full of hungry need.

"Iolanthe. Iolanthe. Do you want to come?" His words are ragged, his tone husky. "Shall I make you come, my wife?"

I pump my hips over him, working my body against his hand. As I do, I can feel the heated length of his cock between us, dribbles of his seed glazing my skin where I've brushed against him. It reminds me that there's a bigger goal here, and that if he makes me come first, we might not finish. He's not nearly as keen on deflowering me ahead of our wedding as I am.

So I shake my head and give his lower lip a fierce nip. "Want you inside me. I can take it."

"I know you can, sweet love," he groans. "Gods, I know you can. I just want you to be sure—"

"I'm sure. I'm very sure, Agakor. Please."

He makes a pained sound, pressing his forehead to mine. "Gods, I don't deserve you."

"But you have me anyhow," I tease. "So make me yours already."

Laughter huffs out of him and he gives my clit one last final rub before slipping his fingers out of me. I immediately feel bereft, wanting to whine in protest at losing that strange, pressing fullness. But then he's kissing me again, and his hands are on my buttocks as he lifts me up and spreads me wide.

Then I feel him, pressing against the most intimate part of my body, the entrance to my womb. He's thick and hot and invasive and just the head of him pushing there makes me squirm with pure lust. "Please," I moan. "Oh please."

"Go slow," he warns me, teeth gritted. "Sink down onto me."

Oh. He wants me to take control? I shift my weight on my knees, my insides clenching at the press of his cock against my entrance. Bearing down against such a large, hard thing doesn't seem as if it'll work. But Agakor is patient, holding me locked in place as he presses kisses to my face and lets me wiggle and squirm over him, trying to figure out the logistics of how our bodies will come together.

Then, he slips inside me. Just a notch, but enough to steal my breath away. Everything's tight, tight, tight…but then he twitches against me, and I'm reminded of before, when my body accommodated his fingers. So I wait, living for his kisses, and when a few moments pass, I give an experimental rock of my hips. Better. I feel as full as before, with his fingers. Maybe even fuller. It's…indescribable. "Are you in?"

Agakor makes an indecipherable sound.

Is that…a no? I reach between us, and I feel my body,

stretched tight around him. Moving my fingers lower, I realize I've only managed to swallow the head of him inside my body. Oh. Goddess Belara, he has a *lot* of cock. But I'm determined. "I can take it," I tell him.

"You can." His voice is strained. "I know you can. Just relax and let it happen."

Relax? Let it happen? He's not the one trying to take something as big as my forearm into his body. Panting, I try to do as he asks, though. I close my eyes and do my best to relax, leaning into his kisses and dragging the tips of my breasts over his chest as I move. His hips move in short, rocking motions as we share small, quick kisses.

"Touch yourself," he tells me. "Right on your clit. Make yourself feel good."

I bury my face against his neck in shyness. "Right now?"

"Aye, right now. Show it to me."

Oh, goddess. With a whimper, I place a trembling hand between my thighs and caress myself there. Immediately, lust flickers through my body. With him pressing into me, it adds another layer of sensation, and I whimper again as I continue to toy with my clit. All the breath seems to have left my body, and as he murmurs words of encouragement, I keep teasing myself.

"Look at how good you are," he croons, and the fine hairs on my neck stand up. Gods, he sounds so amazing when he talks to me like that. "Look at how much of my cock you're taking into that tight little cunt of yours, Iolanthe. Keep going. You can take more."

"I can," I pant, desperately wanting to please him. It feels like I'm at the limit of what my body can take, but somehow I keep shifting my hips and touching myself, and I sink further down onto him. My thighs brush against his and I realize how much of him is inside me. He lifts his hands and I sink down the rest of the way with a gasp, sheathing him entirely. "Oh, goddess."

"Beautiful," Agakor says, his hand going to the back of my neck and pulling me in for another kiss. "You are so beautiful, Iolanthe. So perfect. How do you feel?"

"Really full," I manage. Everything feels tight and stuffed and like nothing I've felt before.

He kisses me again, and one hand slides to my breast. "Just relax. Get used to the feeling, love."

Oh. He's calling me love? My heart does a happy little dance at the nickname. I smile up at him, but I quickly grow distracted again as his thumb moves over my nipple, teasing and toying with it until it's aching and I'm dying to move on top of him. With a frustrated sound, I rock my hips…and nothing hurts. It's still tight, still a lot, but I can handle this. "Agakor," I say, smiling as I slide my arms around his neck. "What do we do now?"

"Now," he tells me in a low voice. "You hold on and let me claim you."

Hold on? But his meaning becomes clear when he clasps my hips and lifts me up off of him, high enough that only the tip of his cock remains inside me. Then, he drags me back down over his length, until I'm engulfing him once more. Oooh. After a few rounds of this, I tentatively start to move with him, wanting to participate. It increases the friction between us, and the pleasure, and it takes me a few moments to realize we're moving so fast that I'm practically bouncing atop him as he works me over his cock. It feels good, but it's not quite the same as when his hand was on my clit. I don't have that intense lightning bolt of pleasure that makes my toes curl. This just feels…nice. Deep and different, but nice.

Agakor hums in his throat, the sound curious and thoughtful, as if he's just figured something out. I want to ask him what it is, but he changes the angle on his next thrust, dragging me down against him hard, and I gasp. That felt…different. Something hot and needy unfurls in my belly. "Oh."

"That's better," he murmurs. "You like that, sweetheart?"

I nod, holding onto him as he rocks into me again, and once more, that deep slide of him into my body seems to strike an entirely different, far more sensitive spot. Pleasure pools in my belly—different than the lightning of his hand on my clit, but something I need to pursue. "More," I tell him. "I need more of that."

"Aye?" he asks, voice husky. "That feels good, doesn't it? Hitting the spot now?" When I nod frantically, he thrusts again, and then he's moving quickly, pumping into me faster than before. My breath comes in hitching gasps as I try to match his rhythm, but it's hard for me to follow when he keeps striking that spot inside me. I forget all about being cold or how big he feels pressing into me, and I chase that curling thread of pleasure. I dig my nails into his skin and bear down on him as he pushes upward.

On and on, and that sweet, elusive pleasure keeps building. I sob with need, driving myself down on him as he pushes into me. I might be begging. I might be slamming my hips down on his. I might be touching myself frantically—all I know is that I have to come, and desperately. I press my face to his neck, focused, and I'm shocked when he bites down on my shoulder. The hot, hard nip of it startles me—and then I'm coming harder than I've ever come before, my legs jerking as wave after wave of release unleashes through me. Agakor whispers in my ear and tells me how beautiful I am even as he drives into me again and again, teasing more of the release out of me.

I slump against him, boneless and sated, and he growls low in his throat. "Can I put you on your back, love?" I nod, and then his arms are on my back and he's over me in the cave. I'm laying atop our cast-aside clothing and my backside is on the cold cave floor, but it doesn't seem to matter. I'm too dazed to move as Agakor pushes my knees up practically to my shoulders and then mounts me again, driving into me so hard that his balls slap against my skin. When he comes, it's with a dark snarl, his big body shuddering over mine. He drives into me once, twice more, and then falls over me, caging me with his arms.

Slowly, I become aware of just how heavy he is. I sigh, sliding my hand over his arm, not wanting to spoil the moment. "There's a rock pushing into my backside," I whisper. "Can we sit up?"

He chuckles, the sound exhausted but pleased, and lifts off of me. Immediately, I feel the loss of his body over mine, and I'm extremely aware of the sticky wetness between my thighs. Oh, Belara's mercy, we made a *mess*. I slide a hand between my thighs and his seed is everywhere. "Please tell me there's a towel somewhere in this cave."

"No, but I have a tunic." He pulls me to my feet and cleans me off, and I inwardly cringe at what everyone is going to think when he shows up tomorrow with no tunic on. Will they know what we were doing?

Then again, it *is* our wedding night. Sort of. "So what happens now?"

He pulls me close, pressing a kiss to my cheek and then nipping at my ear. He's affectionate even now, and I move closer into his arms, pressing against his bare skin. It feels good to let him cuddle me after everything we just did, even though my knees feel like they're made of water. "Does something more need to happen?" He tongues my earlobe. "Do you want me to make you come again? I can."

"Do we stay here all night?" I clarify, blushing. "Do you still need to club me?"

Agakor kisses me again, pressing his mouth along my jaw. "I'm not clubbing you. They'll be able to smell that we were together and draw their conclusions from there."

I bite back a moan of dismay. His people do things differently, I remind myself. "I guess we could show them the bite you put on my shoulder if someone really needs proof."

He puts a finger under my chin, angling my face up. "They won't need to see it. They'll be able to see the nips I left all over your throat. I think I got a little carried away." He holds me against him, stroking a hand up and down my back. "Are you sore anywhere?" When I shrug, he chuckles down at me. "You will be tomorrow, mark my words."

"Tomorrow, when I'm supposed to escape you?" I point out.

"I'll let you give me a love-tap with the club," he promises. "My father will be thrilled to see it." Then he's kissing me again, his arms tight around me. "My bride. My sweet Iolanthe. Sometimes I still can't believe you want me."

"You *paid* for a bride," I point out, laughing.

"I did. And I expected to drag my grudging woman to the altar. To have you is just…a gift beyond imagining." He tucks me against him, and I feel safe and protected. "I should regret what we did tonight. That we didn't wait for our wedding night. But I'm so glad, Iolanthe. So damned glad."

"I am too. Knowing our luck, someone would have shown up with a long-lost Novoran relative and want to perform yet another marriage ceremony," I grumble.

Agakor laughs, his big body shaking with delight. "You've heard that Novorans believe in wife-sharing, haven't you?"

Scandalized, I lightly smack his stomach. "They do not. You're teasing me."

"It's true. They're an odd people." His big hand smooths down my hair. "Are you sure you have no regrets, love?"

"Are you sure that I'm your 'love'?" I lob back, teasing him. "We only just met less than a fortnight ago."

His fingers snarl in a tangle, and I wince, but he continues to stroke my hair, gently working through the knot, and I decide I like this. Being petted after sex is almost as nice as the sex. Almost. Agakor is amused at my question, though. "You think it's too soon for me to love you? How much time do you think I need?"

"More than this?"

"Mmm, I disagree. Orcs love very quickly. We can become attached at a glance. My father fell in love with my mother when he attacked her encampment and she nearly gutted him with a meat-skewer. He says right then it was love. As for me…"

His knuckles brush over the swell of my breasts. "I'd love to say it was the moment I saw your freckles, but it wasn't."

"When was it?" I ask, curious. What was the moment that decided me for him? When my gown was torn off? When he "tasted" me? Some other moment in the last week or so?

The amusement in his voice is like a warm blanket as he leans close and whispers in my ear. "When you petted my cock. You were unafraid and fascinated, and you clearly had no idea what you were doing. In that moment, I fell in love."

I make an indignant sound in my throat, but I ruin my outrage by giggling. I can only imagine how it must have seemed to him. I don't remember how I touched it, but I know I didn't use the tight, firm circling grip he likes when we met for our solar rendezvous. "Was it bad?"

"Incredibly awkward," he agrees. "But so charming." He plants a kiss atop my head. "Just like my bride."

Iolanthe

The rest of the wedding ceremonies go off without a hitch. The next morning, Mudag announces that we're married in the eyes of his clan, and Agakor immediately calls back the priest of Belara. That evening, we have our second wedding and the accompanying feast, and spend our first officially married night in bed together. Now that I'm officially Agakor's wife, I turn the keep-cleaning into high gear, hiring extra servants from the nearby town. We scrub the place inside out, and then I set about to decorating. It turns out that Turnip knows everyone in town and is a fantastic haggler, so I make her the "official" housekeeper. When I hand her a set of keys, she gets misty-eyed and sniffs, though she denies it.

Nights with Agakor are perfection. He takes the time to make me come at least twice before he takes his own release, and I love exploring him and trying out new things in bed. It's all exciting to me, and I still can't believe he finds me so attractive. He can't keep his hands off of me, touching me when we're at dinner, or insisting I sit in his lap while I read a book by the fire. I eat it up, though. After years of being ignored and lonely, I love my grabby, affectionate husband.

Life would be perfect…if only my father weren't determined to destroy things.

Agakor tells me not to worry about it. That he won't let anything happen to me. That he won't let my father take me from him. I trust him—I do—but it hurts me when I see new mercenaries arriving at our keep every day. It concerns me that Agakor and his men are constantly scouting and looking for my father's spies. I know my father won't give up.

It's not about me. He's using that as a pretense, a justification to attack Agakor because he's wealthy. He's not concerned about my happiness. The only thing my father has ever been concerned with is his own coin and power. My sisters and I were just useful tools to help him grow that power. Now that he sees an easy avenue to increase his wealth again, he will stop at nothing to get Agakor's treasury.

It worries me. And after I have been married a week, word trickles down that my father is in talks with a neighboring lord. That concerns me more than anything else. Agakor has men, but he doesn't have the reputation. What if the local lords band together and approach the king, asking him to step in? My father could easily fabricate a story about how I'd been kidnapped and that I'm being held against my will. If he musters the support of his neighbors and they attack en masse? Not even Agakor has enough men to hold back an army.

I confess my fears in bed that night, after another round of lovemaking. "You just don't know my father like I do," I fret when he tries to soothe me. "Papa is like a bull with his head down when he gets an idea. He knows you're wealthy and he thinks he can take it."

Agakor rubs my back, his fingers trailing up and down my bare spine. I'm curled up against him, naked, my cheek on his chest, one hand possessively cupping his sac because I love touching him intimately. I'm growing as possessive of him as he is of me. "You worry too much, love. Let me take care of it."

"But I know what he's capable of," I protest. "He'll scheme his way to get his hands on your coin."

"No one can take it from me, Iolanthe. They cannot take you. They cannot take my funds. I will go to war to protect you. Trust in that."

I frown, because I don't want him going to war. I don't want any of this. I just want to have a quiet life with my wonderful husband. I need to talk to my father directly, I decide. If he has a scrap of affection for me, maybe he'll listen. Immediately, I begin planning what I must do. Horses, I decide, since woales are slow. I'll need men to go with me, as well—

"Iolanthe?" Agakor asks, twirling one long strand of my hair around his finger. "You're too quiet. Tell me what you're thinking."

Already he knows me too well. I roll his sac in my hand, teasing his balls as I look up at him and give him a sultry smile. "I was thinking that we need to work on me getting pregnant.

Then there can be no question about anything."

His eyes light up, and he grins. "I love the way you think, wife."

"I love it when you call me wife," I purr back, sitting up and slinging my leg over his hips. Tomorrow, I decide. Tomorrow I'll ride out and talk to my father. Tonight is for my husband.

The next morning, I kiss my husband a dozen times in the courtyard, weepy.

Agakor just chuckles, holding me close. "We're only going one town over, love. I'll be back by tomorrow afternoon, I promise. I just want to make sure that all the mercenaries in the area know that I'm looking for more trained men, and that I pay well. You'll be safe here in the keep."

"I know," I sniff. My head is full of my plans, which could be dangerous. It's not hard to be upset. What if I meet my father and he refuses to let me go back to Agakor? I won't let that happen, I decide. Digging my fingers into Agakor's tunic, I stand on my tiptoes and kiss his chin. "I'll miss you, though. So much."

"If you need anything, Tindal will help you," he promises me. "Just ask him."

"I will."

He pauses, gazing down at me. "You make me so happy, Iolanthe. Don't let your father's saber-rattling worry you, all right? Let me take care of you, as a husband should."

"Of course." I smooth out the front of his tunic, since I just wrinkled it. "I love you, too. I hope you have success on your trip. Hurry back soon."

I wait in the courtyard, waving goodbyes until my husband's horses and his men are out of sight. He's leaving with a small band—worrisome—but I understand why. He wants the rest to remain here at the keep, protecting it. Protecting *me*. Well, I can protect my husband, too. I gather my skirts and head inside, looking for Tindal.

I find him in the cellar, overlooking the delivery of several barrels of ale. He immediately gets a wary look on his face as I march towards him. "Uh oh," Tindal says. "I know that look. That's the look Agakor wears when he wants something and he knows I hate the idea."

Am I taking on some of my husband's mannerisms, then? I find the idea pleasing. "I have a favor to ask."

"Of course you do." He eyes the men carrying barrels in, wincing as one is set on the floor with a loud thud. "If you spill it, I still have to buy it," he warns the man. "Don't cost me good coin!"

I wait until the barrel is settled and then turn to Tindal. "I need several men and a few fast horses."

He blanches. "Do I want to ask why?"

I consider lying. If Agakor was here, he'd stop me. He'd throw me over his shoulder and take me to bed and lick me until I'm writhing with pleasure and every single thought has flown out of my mind. But my actions are to protect him, just like they are to protect the home we're building here. So I decide to tell Tindal the truth. "My father is feeling out other lords and I'm worried he's going to get too many people on his side. If he rouses the entire countryside, it won't matter that Agakor bought this keep fair and square, or that he paid my father a wagonful of coin to marry me. They'll see a half-orc interloper and that's it. So I mean to go and have a nice long talk with my father and make it very clear that I'm here by choice."

Tindal stares at me.

"What?" I ask.

"I can't decide if you're crazy or a genius."

"A little of both?" I give him a wary smile. "I'm not sure how it's going to go, but at least I can try."

He gnaws on his upper lip, his green-skinned face contorting. "Normally I'd say fuck no, but I have a feeling you're going to do this either way, aren't you?" At my nod, he sighs. "Then let me settle these barrels, and we'll get you some fast horses and the most loyal men Agakor has." He hesitates and then looks at me again. "If you don't come back in one piece, just know that he's going to have my head on a pike."

"It'll be fine," I reassure him. "It's my father. He won't harm me."

The look he gives me is downright pitying.

Iolanthe

The soldiers that Tindal sends with me are excellent men. Two of them are half-orc like my husband, one is fully orkish, and the others are human. All are fierce riders and tireless. I'm the one slowing us down, so I do my best to encourage my mare to go faster than I've ever ridden before, and I hold on for dear life. We stop at a small inn overnight and leave at dawn with fresh horses, charging towards my father's land with breakneck speed.

Even though I'd probably be more comfortable in pants, I'm wearing one of my finest dresses. It's an older red one with vibrant skirts and decorative sleeves, and the nearly bare boning in the bodice stabs the underside of my breast every time the horse moves. I ignore it, though, just like I ignore how sore my legs are and how angry Agakor is going to be when he finds out where I've gone. Getting my father to see reason is all that matters. So I wear my oldest, most favorite gown, I braid my hair like I did when I was younger, and I ride at the front of our little party as we head onto the outskirts of my father's land.

I want everyone to know it's me. I want there to be no question in anyone's mind that Lady Iolanthe has arrived to see her father. I make sure we slow down in the village and I wave greetings to everyone, calling several of the people by their names. I know them, just as I know several of them used to work at the keep for my father and no longer do because he stopped paying them. Even the poor have to eat, but my father doesn't care. I'm starting to realize how truly selfish my father is, and it's difficult. Even though I'm upset, he's still my father. He's still the person I'm most familiar with in this world.

Or…he was. Funny how in just a few short weeks I know Agakor better than I know the man I've lived with for thirty years.

Determined, I ride right up the road, heading for Rockmourn Keep. As I head there, I see multiple encampments on my father's lands. Near the road, at the edges of the crop fields, soldiers cluster around campfires. That's concerning. It really does look as if he's enlisting an army. Most of the faces I don't recognize, and the ones I do, I make sure to call out a greeting to. "Thorvald," I call to my father's blacksmith. "How are the children?"

I'm gratified at the look of astonishment on his face.

It doesn't take long for my father's man-at-arms to race

through the camps to meet me. Sir Foyleton marches up, wearing his greaves and vambraces over a mud-stained tunic. He looks flabbergasted to see me as well. I call out a cheery greeting from atop my horse. "Sir Foyleton! You look quite well. My goodness, it's so busy here. Is my father around?"

I give him my brightest, emptiest smile, since I'm a daughter that's known for staying inside by the fire and reading or sewing instead of paying attention to warlike things. If I seem sweet and useless, they'll treat me like such.

He gives the men at my side—all better-armored and far more dangerous-looking than my father's ragtag mercenaries—a scrutinizing look. "What are you doing here?"

"Oh! I heard a terrible rumor that someone was saying that I was being held against my will, so I decided to come and visit my father and reassure him that I'm just fine." I beam at him. "Is he nearby? I'd love to see him."

Sir Foyleton hesitates. "I'm sure he is. Would you like to come to the keep with me, my lady?"

I pat my horse's neck and do my best to look relaxed, even though I'm tired and my backside feels like it's on fire. I know what this plan is. They don't want the men to hear the truth about why my father is picking a fight. If I show up and parade around, I can't very well look like a hostage. Just being here is ruining his plans. So I say, "I'm doing quite well up here. Can't Father come meet me outside? It's a lovely day."

He frowns in my direction. "I'm sure you'd be more comfortable inside."

"I'm sure I wouldn't," I reiterate gently. A new fearful thought hits me—what if I go into my father's keep and he doesn't let me leave? There's no way I'm stepping foot in there. "My husband's men are out here, and I shall stay with them."

Sir Foyleton blusters on. "I'm sure you're all welcome inside—"

"No," I say firmly. "If my father wants to talk to me, he will need to come and greet me out here." Since my tone is sharp, I switch to a benign, vapid smile. "Which I'm sure he will want to do since he was terrified I was being held hostage. It's so strange, that. Why, if he was worried about such a thing, I question why he left me there before seeing to my marriage. Isn't that odd?"

He doesn't meet my eyes. Instead, he flags down a young boy. "You. Go and find Lord Purnav. Tell him that his daughter has returned."

"Visiting," I clarify. "I'm just visiting."

"Visiting," Sir Foyleton chokes out, agreeing.

Keeping the idiot smile on my face, I sit in the sunshine and gaze around me at the soldiers. I don't even know if they can be called soldiers. They don't have uniforms. Their tents are a sorry, muddy mess, and most of them don't seem to have armor. Is my father hiring everyone that shows up and can hold a sword? It makes me furiously angry, but I have to play this carefully. My horse prances in the rutted road, and I glance back at the men accompanying me. They might as well be stone for all the emotion they're showing. The hot sun bearing down doesn't bother them. The stares of the men on the side of the road leave them unfazed. Truly, does my father think he can win against Agakor? There's not a chance. No wonder my husband wasn't worried.

Even so, I don't like the thought of a fight breaking out over me. So I toss my braid back and glance over at Sir Foyleton, who still stands in the middle of the road, as if he's determined to supervise my appearance here. I keep my voice bright and cheery as I loudly ask, "Where have all these men come from?"

Sir Foyleton gives me a quelling look. He doesn't answer me.

That's all right. I don't need him to. I glance at one of my men behind me. One of the half-orcs—Throx—speaks up, cold and succinct. "Mercenaries."

"Mercenaries?" I echo, pretending to be surprised. "But how is that possible? Sir Foyleton, how is my father affording mercenaries? He doesn't have any coin."

Sir Foyleton's eyes bug and his face turns a dark shade of red. He rushes forward, trying to grab the reins of my horse. Alarmed, my mare prances, and there's a jingle of armor. The orc with me, a Broketusk warrior who only answers to "Red," snatches the reins of my mount away from my father's man-at-arms and glares at him. Foyleton retreats, and Red pats the nose of my mare, glancing up at me with a nod.

"Please don't touch my horse," I say sweetly to Sir Foyleton. "She's quite skittish. And you didn't say how my father afforded all these mercenaries when everyone knows he's *quite* poor. Do tell me. I'd love to know."

The knight doesn't answer. He continues to glare at us, waiting for my father's approach. It doesn't matter. I'm here to sow the seeds of doubt. I glance over at the encampments, and some of them are openly staring at me and my accompanying men. There are suspicious looks on their faces. If I can destroy the morale—or even peel some of the mercenaries away from my father's army—I'll consider my job here complete.

"Iolanthe!" My father's angry bellow strikes fear into my heart. For a moment, I'm a gangly young woman again, hunch-ing her shoulders by the fire and trying not to be noticed as my father paces and screams at his steward for spending too much coin. I lift my chin, though my bravado is gone.

Father seems smaller to me today. His appearance hasn't changed, but when I compare him to the men at my back or my big, strong husband, my father seems puny and lacking. His beard is streaked with gray, and from atop my horse I can see the bald spot he tries to hide. His face looks lined and hard and unpleasant, and I wonder what my mother ever saw in him.

"What are you doing here?" he hisses as he approaches my horse.

Red puts a hand out to stop my father before he can march up to my mare and frighten her, and Father shoots a thunderous look in my direction. Inwardly, I cringe, though I do my best to regain the righteous indignation I had before. "I thought you'd be glad to see me," I call out loudly. "Since you're telling everyone that I was kidnapped. You know that's not true, Father. Everyone knows that you sold my hand in marriage to Agakor because he was wealthy and you had no funds to pay your knights."

Father's jaw clenches. He points at the ground, indicating that I should come and stand in front of him, like a naughty child.

For a moment, I'm that cowering young girl. I'm the maiden who wants to sink into the shadows and hide when her father yells, because I know he'll be horrid to live with for the next several days. And I hate myself for it, but I slide off the back of my horse and step forward, ready to do just that.

Red moves in front of me and shakes his head. "Agakor wouldn't like it."

I take a deep breath, and it's like I'm myself again. Right. I don't answer to my father anymore. I have a husband. I can't even say that I answer to him, because truthfully, Agakor gives me my way on everything. So I lift my chin and take a defiant step toward my father, and go no closer. "Don't you want to hug your daughter? Your daughter that you were afraid had been stolen away?"

He scowls at me, holding his ground. "What are you doing here, Iolanthe? Why are you stirring up trouble?"

Me, stirring up trouble? That's rich, coming from him. "I wanted to show you that I'm well. That there's no reason for the army you're mounting to attack my husband. Because that is the plan, isn't it? You're going to attack Agakor under the pretense of my name. I'm here because that's wrong."

Father's lip curls. "He shouldn't be allowed to hold land. He's a bastard half-orc."

"You knew he was a half-orc when you sold me to him in marriage," I point out, ignoring the bastard part. "It seemed to be all right with you then."

"Come inside," Father demands. "I'll put you up in your old room and we'll forget about all of this. You're safe here."

Does he think I'm crawling back to him? My temper flares, and for a moment I'm furiously angry at Father's nerve. He acts as if the truth doesn't exist, and that just infuriates me. "I'm not going anywhere with you," I say, as loud as I can. "You break your word to everyone. You gave me to Agakor in marriage and drove off with his gold before the wedding. You don't get a say in my life any longer."

Father's face contorts with rage. "Iolanthe—"

I talk over him, continuing. "You don't have enough coin

to pay all these men. That's why you're having to go to distant towns to find mercenaries—because the ones from here won't work for you. They know you won't pay them. They know your reputation for being stingy and cheap. That's why all the soldiers have left Rockmourn Keep, Father. They abandoned you because you didn't pay them."

"Lies!"

"I wish they were." I put my hands on my horse's saddle and accept Red's hand as he helps me mount again. My skirts get bunched up around my legs and my backside aches, but I ignore all of it. "I've known you longer than anyone, Father. I wish I could say you had my loyalty, but you tricked me and sold me out just like you're going to sell out these men. Unluckily for you, Agakor is a good, strong leader and he's going to crush you if you try anything." I take the reins of my mount and turn her, facing the encampments clustered along the side of the road. "Unlike my father, my husband is very wealthy. He is also looking for mercenaries. You can ask anywhere—Agakor of Broketusk Clan has an excellent reputation for fair payment. And if you tell him that you left my father's army to join his, I'll ensure that you get paid double what my father has promised."

"Iolanthe!"

I ignore his angry shout. I'm too far in at this point. "Too bad Father's promises are worth nothing," I call out, turning my horse away. "Goodbye, Father. I shall tell my husband you said hello."

There's an angry sputtering behind me as my horse picks up her feet and begins to head back down the road. I can feel all eyes on me. I don't know if my bluff will work, but I think it will. All they have to do is ask questions. I ignore the ache in my heart, because I know Father will hate me now. My sisters might, too. But I've chosen who I side with, and it's the half-orc that treats me like I'm not just a tall, ungainly spinster. He treats me like I'm a goddess.

"Seize her," my father cries out. "Someone grab her! Bring her into the keep!"

My shoulders stiffen. My father isn't really going to try this, is he? I urge my mare onward, tense and waiting for someone to attack. Instead, I hear someone call out, "Is what she said true?"

Another demands, "I want my coin up front!"

It's something. Biting back my smile, I keep riding and I don't look back.

No one tries to stop me.

Agakor

No horse is fast enough. No matter how much I push my mount, it's never quite as fast as the frantic beat of my heart as I race to save my new wife from her father's clutches. I can't stop my horse, not even for a moment. Once I returned to Cragshold and Tindal confessed Iolanthe's plan, I rode out immediately. We've ridden through the night as well, swapping our tired mounts for fresh horses at an inn. Even now, my mount struggles to keep the bruising pace I've set, but I refuse to slow down. Every time I close my eyes, I see sweet, innocent Iolanthe, greeting her father with open arms and her father shoving her behind the doors of his keep, never to be seen again. I picture her tears as she realizes that her father won't release her. I imagine how sad she'll be to leave my side, and how she'll feel responsible.

I know her. I know her soft heart…and that's why I urge my steed even though he's lathered and flagging. I have to do something, and fast.

"Agakor," one of the men calls to me. It's Haster, a rough-looking ex-mercenary who's ridden at my side for years now. He points up ahead. "Riders headed this way."

Someone mutters and makes the sign to ward off evil. Haster has pale, inhuman-looking eyes and can see farther than anyone should be able to. There's a lot of rumors about him being sired from one of the gods, and unlucky, but I've known him long enough that such things don't bother me. I draw up short, my riders following my lead, and we wait.

I put a hand to my sword as my horse blows out a winded breath, and assess my surroundings. Rockmourn Keep is located squarely in the most barren part of Adassia, and our surroundings are nothing but gently rolling hills tumbled with rock and strewn with weeds. The road here is hard and dry, rutted from hundreds of wagons crossing it over the years, and there's not a single tree to be found. In the distance, at the top of a hill, I finally see a faint plume of dust—the riders Haster warned about.

I tense, counting shapes. Two…three…four… If it's a war party, we can take them out, though I don't like the thought of spilling blood first. They're not going to stop me from retrieving my wife, however. Nothing will. If I have to burn down Lord Purnav and his keep to get her back, I will.

Six…seven…eight. Not a war party, then. A band of scouts?

Outriders? My fingers dance on the pommel of my sword as the black dots become shapes on horseback. Somewhere behind me, Haster chuckles…and then I see red. Bright red skirts.

Hot relief pours through me, even as I urge my mount forward, riding toward her. As I do, I pick up her delicate scent in the air. She smells like herself and like sweat, and there's a hint of campfires and mud, but nothing else.

Good. Then no one's touched her. No one's harmed her or tried to stop her.

I ride right up to Iolanthe's horse and snag her from the saddle, pulling her into my arms. She makes an adorable squeak and clings to me. "Agakor!"

Her nose is sunburned and her hair is frizzy from riding, but she's beautiful. So very beautiful. I press a kiss to the side of her head as I turn my mount and start riding back in the direction of my lands. "I am so damned furious at you for this stunt," I growl. "I should pull you over my knee and spank you."

Iolanthe lets out an indignant gasp as one of the men chuckles. Her escorts file in with my men, and I'm pleased to see Red and Throx with her. Both of them are good, loyal men and I know Tindal sent the best with her, since he couldn't stop her. I'm still mad, though. Mad that my headstrong little bride put herself in danger. Mad that she came so close to being snatched out of my grasp.

I'm definitely going to spank her the moment we're alone. That little gasp and the wiggle she gave in my lap indicated she was titillated by the idea. So she's definitely getting spanked… but only if she wants it.

"You can't be mad at me," Iolanthe insists as she settles in my arms. "I had to show myself. If my father's telling them I'm a hostage, I've shown everyone that he's lying. I showed them that I'm free and happy in my marriage." She hesitates, and then adds, "And I mentioned very loudly that he was broke and that you'd pay anyone that defected double what he's offering."

Throwing back my head, I laugh in sheer delight at Iolanthe's cleverness. Not only did she parade herself about to make a fool of her father, but she's undermining his troops under his nose. I love it.

"Did I do good, then?" my wife asks, preening under my approval. "It was an excellent plan, don't you think?"

I lean in and nip at her ear, my voice a growling whisper. "I'm still going to spank you later."

Her breath catches and her hands spasm against my tunic. Yes, she definitely likes that idea.

"Agakor," Haster calls again. When I turn to him, he indicates behind us. "Men headed this way on foot."

"How many?"

He squints at the distant horizon. "Three. No…four."

Too few to be a war party. They're defecting already, then. I still want to shake Iolanthe for risking herself, but I squeeze her tighter against me. "Your plan was a good one," I agree. "And now you have to promise me you will never, ever do anything like that again. It's not that I don't trust you. It's that I don't trust your father."

She nods, sliding her hands to the front of my tunic and rubbing my chest in the way she does when she's aroused. "You'll just have to give me a baby so it's out of the question."

I bite back a feral growl of pleasure. We're still hours away from the nearest town that I trust, and I won't be able to ride if my cock is stiff. But I can't resist whispering to my wife, "We're stopping at an inn tonight and I'm going to fill you with my seed over and over again. I'm going to breed you, my pretty little freckled wife."

She slings her arms around my neck. "I can't wait to get to the inn." Then, she leans in and confides, "My arse is killing me."

I don't stop laughing for leagues.

We finally make it to a decent-looking inn, a safe distance from Purnav's land. It's dark by the time we arrive, and Iolanthe is curled against my chest, dozing. I rouse her and we head inside, with my men agreeing to guard our horses in shifts.

"And to have a nice chat with the defectors heading this way," Throx adds cheerfully. "Because there's bound to be more coming."

I nod, carrying my sleepy bride inside the inn. She's not used to so much riding and she's completely depleted, barely stirring as I get a room and haul her up the stairs. The innkeeper opens the door to his finest room for me and it's a decent one, with a large feather bed and pleasant-looking wood furniture. He bites my coin furtively to make sure that it's real, but that doesn't even faze me. All I care about is getting Iolanthe settled.

When my wife is tucked into bed and sleeping, I head back downstairs and grab a bite to eat. I check in on my men, and sure enough Throx and Red are both talking to a band of what look to be at least twenty of the scraggly mercenaries from Lord Purnav's ragtag army. I have a feeling that Iolanthe's little plan is going to give her father a great deal of trouble, and I couldn't be prouder of my clever wife. Thinking of her, I get a few cold meat pies and a pitcher of honeyed ale and bring them upstairs with me so she'll have something to eat when she wakes.

Iolanthe is sitting up in bed when I return, however. Her hair is spilling over her shoulders and she rubs her sleepy face with a dazed expression. "Where are we?"

"Inn in Lagoros," I tell her. "A bit off path, but clean and safe. Are you hungry?"

She nods and takes a meat pie from me. "You're so thoughtful, Agakor. Thank you so much."

I'm not thoughtful. I'm an absolute rutting monster who's just trying to be patient as I watch my tired wife nibble at a meat pie and take a few sips of ale. She's eating slowly, her shoulders drooping with exhaustion, and I'm still going to plow her sweet cunt tonight and fill her with my seed, because I need to claim her. Need to make her realize that she belongs to me and me alone. Need to put a baby inside her so no one else can ever think of taking my wife from me.

I twitch in the chair across from her as she takes small bites. I need to do something or else I'm going to flip her over and drive into her from behind while she licks the gravy off her fingers. So I get to my feet and go to the washbasin, pouring water into it. I move to Iolanthe's side and pick at the intricate knots on her sleeves, undressing her as she eats. "I can get that," she protests as I tug the laces free on one sleeve and then move to the other. "You don't have to undress me."

"I do, or I'm never going to get your naked," I grumble. "You eat too slow."

Her giggle of amusement warms my belly. "I'm sorry. I can't eat as fast as you. My mouth is smaller."

"I like your small mouth. And your small hands."

This time, she snorts with laughter. "I do *not* have small hands. Nothing on me is dainty."

"Your hands are small on my cock," I say, leaning in to kiss her. She tastes like meat pie and ale, and when I lift my mouth from hers, she looks dazed and distracted. "Are you done eating?"

"It's because your cock is so great in size," Iolanthe agrees, holding the pie out for me to take. "It would dwarf any woman's hands."

Well now, she knows how to flatter a man.

I take the last of the pie from her and set it aside, then help her pull off the constricting red dress and attached bodice. Women's clothes are a damned nightmare as far as I'm concerned, and I want her to be comfortable. When she's in nothing but her chemise, she scratches at her waist and sighs pleasantly. "Much better."

I'm not done with her yet, though. I get a cloth, dip it in the washbasin, and then wipe down her hands, face, neck and feet, much to Iolanthe's amusement. She protests that I'm treating her like a child, but she doesn't push me away, which tells me just how tired she truly is. Iolanthe is exhausted, even though she's fighting it. That's all right. For this next part, all she has to do is lie back and let me make her feel good. So once she's clean, I toss the washcloth into the basin, push my mate's chemise up to her waist, and begin kissing along the insides of her thighs.

"Oh," Iolanthe breathes, her toes curling. She lies back on the bed, her long hair loose, a dreamy expression on her face. "Oh, are we doing that?"

"Should I stop? Are you too tired?" I kiss up to her knee, lifting it as I go.

"Too tired to have you do all the work?" She chuckles, hitching her chemise up a little higher and revealing her pretty cunt to me. "Not at all. Your mouth feels good."

I grin up at her. "Then let me take care of you in this way, too." And I kiss my way up to the apex of her parted thighs.

She makes sweet little sighs as I settle between her legs, propping them over my shoulders. I immediately set to work, tonguing her in the way I know she likes. Iolanthe squirms against my tongue, her hand sliding to my hair as I lavish attention on her folds. She hums with pleasure as I work her clit, sucking and teasing it, but I can tell she needs a bit more tonight. She's tired and it's taking her longer to get aroused. That's all right. Normally I'd feast on her for hours, content to just spend my time between her legs, but I know she's fatigued. I've been saving one of my tricks for a special occasion, and now seems like a good opportunity.

So I ease a finger into her warmth, even as I continue to lap at her clit. She makes another humming sound of pleasure, so I add another finger, stretching her for my cock. She's wet, but not slippery enough to take me with ease. Not yet. I crook my finger inside her, searching for the slightly roughened spot inside her front wall. It takes a moment to find it, but when I do, the reaction is immediate. Iolanthe's legs jerk and she sucks in a breath. "W-what was that?"

"Nothing love," I murmur against her flesh. "Lie back and enjoy."

Iolanthe's hand tightens in my hair, and I notice the other is twisted in the front of her chemise. She likes to pull and tug on her clothing when she's in danger of losing control, and the sight of this pleases me. I tickle my finger at the spot inside her even as I suck on her clit again, and she cries out, arching against my mouth.

Loving her reaction, I tongue her with enthusiasm, determined to wring every little cry and gasp out of her. Every bit of this is perfection, from the way her heels dig into my back as she strains against my fingers, to the wet sounds her cunt is now making as I tease a stroking finger in and out before teasing her rough spot again. She squeals, and then my name is a needy, high-pitched whine in her throat as her hips quiver and jerk, her release looming closer and closer.

When her legs tighten against my face, I can ignore my own need no longer. I lift my head—immediately, Iolanthe cries a protest and tries to shove my head back down. "No!"

"I'm going to come inside you," I promise her, untangling from her clinging limbs as I tug my belt off and shove my pants down to my knees, freeing my cock. I grab my pretty wife, flushed and trembling underneath me, and lift one of her long, glorious legs straight into the air, pressing her heel to my shoulder. Iolanthe needs a deep angle to stroke inside her properly, and this will give me the leverage I need to make her come, and come hard. I tease the head of my cock at the entrance to her body, and there's only the slightest bit of resistance before she's taking me, bit by bit, into her welcoming body.

Iolanthe moans, her foot pressing against my shoulder as I grip her thigh and slowly rock into her. "Agakor. Please, love. I need you so badly."

"You need me to fill you with my child?" I croon.

"Yes," she sobs. "Give me your baby. Fill me with your seed.

Please!"

It's so out of character for my shy wife to beg in such a way. It makes me crazy with desire, too. Unable to control myself, I surge deep, pumping into her with hard, sure strokes. She cries out with every thrust inside her, her head thrown back and her eyes closed as she revels in the sensations. Her breasts bounce enticingly under her chemise as I pound into her, and with my free hand, I reach out and caress one. I can feel her cunt tightening around me, fluttering as she builds up to her release, and it makes me drive into her faster, harder, my body demanding release. Need to claim her, the primal, orc part of me demands. Need to fill her. Need to impregnate her.

Need to show the world that she's mine.

Iolanthe's climax is so hard she cries out, and her cunt grips me like a vise as the release blazes through her. I drive into her harder, pushing her into the mattress as I surge and surge over her soft body. *Mine. Mine. Mine.* When I come, it's glorious. I spill inside her, the release so scorching and sudden that I see stars in front of my eyes. My balls seem to empty forever, pouring my life into the cradle of her body, until I collapse over her on the bed, spent and breathless.

She strokes my hair, making little sounds of pleasure as she catches her breath. It takes me a moment longer to recover, and when I sit up, I realize just how wet the join of our bodies is. I truly did seed her well, the proof of my need trickling out of her body and dampening her thighs. Automatically, I drag my fingers through the mess and push them back inside her, determined to give her every droplet. "Did I hurt you?"

Iolanthe laughs, as if the question is a silly one. "Of course not."

"I must always ask. I'm so much bigger than you." I rub her legs, pleased at the dazed smile on her face. "You know I plan on doing that again soon, don't you?" When she raises an eyebrow at me, I grin. "I meant what I said. You're not leaving this bed until I breed you."

"That's crude of you to say," she fusses, but the smile on her face and the flush in her cheeks tells me she likes my crude words.

"So you're objecting to my statement, but not to staying in bed for several days?" I tease, and I like it when she hides her face with one of the pillows. So maidenly and shy, even now, with my fingers stroking my seed back into her body. "Very well then. I shall use flowery words to describe just how full I'm going to stuff this pretty little cunt over the next while."

She makes an outraged sound, shaking her head under the pillow she keeps pressed to her pink cheeks. "Agakor! What will your men say?"

"They will say I am lucky," I tell her, teasing my sloppy fingers through her heat again. I find the rough spot on her inner wall and stroke it, and her legs twitch in response yet again. "They will say they do not blame me."

"What of the ones just joining your men?" she asks, the pillow muffling her words. "The ones leaving my father?"

"This will give them time to catch up." I stroke her sweet spot again. "And time for my men to clothe and train them, since they're clearly a waste of good coin. Your father's army is a joke, by the way."

Iolanthe lowers the pillow, her face flushed even as she parts her thighs a little wider for me to continue petting her there. "He's got a bad reputation for paying them. Anyone that has worked for him in the past never comes back. They know better. Now all he can get are inexperienced knights, but enough of them can still be a problem." She bites her lip, her eyes fluttering closed as her neck strains and her hips arch against my hand. "Agakor…wait…"

"Wait for what?" I purr, pleased that she's already getting aroused again.

"Shouldn't we clean up first?"

I shake my head, sliding my dripping fingers out of her equally wet cunt and teasing them over her clit. "When I'm about to fill you again, love? There's no point." I roll her clit between wet fingers and her face contorts with pleasure. "You're ready for me again anyhow, aren't you?"

"Oh, goddess Belara," she pants as I guide myself between her thighs again.

It's a good prayer, I decide. Belara would be well pleased at our lusty efforts. I add my prayer to hers and then send one up to Gental, Lord of Family, and ask that he blesses us, too.

Epilogue

Iolanthe

Three Months Later

Sitting by the fire in the great hall, I'm doing my best to concentrate on my sewing, but it's proving difficult. My chair is comfortable, I have enough light to see by thanks to the cozy fire blazing nearby, and my stomach has settled from this morning's heavings. It's just that I can't help but overhear the crude jokes that Turnip is telling Hogar nearby. She's loud. Very loud. And in typical Turnip fashion, she's crude.

The gray-haired orc watches Turnip with fascination as the washerwoman-now-housekeeper gesticulates wildly. "So she took the men's coin and said, aye, I can do that! Took them three melons and stuffed them up her twat—"

"Turnip," I cry out, face burning. I set down my sewing in my lap and give her an exasperated look.

She wrinkles her nose at me, as if just now realizing I'm overhearing her. Ironic, since she's loud enough for her voice to carry down the halls. "Sorry, m'lady." She leans in towards Hogar. "Three melons and stuffed them right into her cunny. Walked right out the door with 'em and won the bet."

I sigh, giving up. It's impossible to make a lady out of Turnip. Not that I've tried, since we try not to enforce titles too much at Cragshold. Agakor is officially Lord of Cragshold and its lands according to King Mathior, but my husband prefers to simply be Agakor of Broketusk. Unless we're meeting with the other human lords. Then he uses his title, if only to shove it into the faces of the others who look down on him.

Turnip gives Hogar a wink. "I'll save my dirty jokes for later, Hogger. You come back and see me when you're done with your patrol."

"You know I will," the orc tells her, grinning.

Shaking my head, I pick up my sewing again. Hogar leaves, and Turnip flops down in the lord's chair next to the fire across from me. "He's a good male, that one. Generous with his mouth, too."

"Turnip, please." I have to bite the inside of my cheek to keep from smiling. I'm so telling Agakor about this later. "And his name is Hogar, not Hogger."

"Y'ain't seen him without his kilt on, have you? Biggest prick I've ever seen. He likes that I call him Hogger." She gives me a lewd grin.

Oh dear. I think I've just learned far more about Hogar than I ever wanted to. "I'm trying to sew," I protest. "I need to concentrate."

"Look at you, so busy with your sewing," Turnip says, leaning back on the cushions and folding her hands over her belly. "Is that all you do is sew and read?"

I give her a cross look and she chortles. We both know very well that I don't get much time to sit and sew lately. There's too much to do with the running of the keep. Between myself and Tindal and Turnip, we get it covered, but there's always a menu to be planned, cleaning to be organized, linens to be aired, books to be balanced, supplies to be ordered—and everyone checks in with me on everything. I like being part of all of it, but just yesterday Agakor protested that I was working too hard and Tindal and Turnip needed to take on more duties.

So here I am, sitting and sewing today instead of inspecting the newest shipment of cheeses and wine from Yshrem. "I'm letting seams out on my dresses," I tell Turnip. "Rather than buying new ones entirely."

"Shoulda let your man just buy you new ones," she grumbles. "I would have."

"He tried," I admit, sewing a neat stitch into the worn fabric. "But I like sewing, and it doesn't make sense to get new clothes when I'm about to have a baby."

Turnip sits upright, a look of disgust on her face. "That baby's not coming for at least six more months. Spend some coins, damn. I would."

I just shake my head again and go back to sewing. The truth is, I like modifying my own dresses. It makes the fact that I'm having a baby feel more real than just buying new gowns, since

I'm adjusting my existing world to the new life growing inside me. It makes me happy. I run a hand down my belly, which is just now starting to get hard and swell. It's early, I think, but Agakor is a big man and he says that women pregnant with orcs show early. I imagine I'm going to get as big as a house, but the thought is an exciting one instead of frightening.

Turnip flings herself out of the chair and heads off, grumbling about checking in on "Hogger," who hasn't even been gone for more than five minutes. She's got a paramour, which is sweet. I'm happy that she's finding a new contentment in life. Turnip has confessed to me that her first husband was a drunk that beat her and her children have all moved away, so I'm glad she has Cragshold and Hogger—

Oh gods, now *I'm* calling him Hogger.

I sew for a bit longer when I hear voices coming down the hall. One is louder than the others, and full of laughter, and just hearing Agakor's amusement makes my heart swell. I put my sewing in the basket next to my chair and rise to my feet to greet my husband as he enters the great hall.

The moment the doors open, Agakor searches for me. He rushes forward the moment he sees me, shaking his head. "Sit, sit love. You're tired."

"I just stood up," I protest, laughing. "Can't I stand up for five minutes without you panicking?"

He immediately kneels before me on the floor, pressing his cheek to my belly. His arms go around my waist. "Not if it means you disturb my strapping son."

"Or daughter," I point out.

"Or strapping daughter," he agrees happily. His ear is against my belly. "Have you felt anything yet?"

I run my hands through his hair, amused. He's like a child waiting for a holiday when it comes to this baby. "I'm told it'll be a few more weeks before I start to feel anything, alas."

Agakor grunts with disappointment and presses a kiss to my ever-so-slightly rounded belly. "I will be patient, then."

"Will you?" I tease. "That doesn't sound like you." I watch as he gets to his feet, smiling. "Did you meet my father's messengers?"

My big, burly husband sits down in his chair and pulls me gently into his lap. He wraps his arms around me, tucking me against him, and I should really protest at how heavy I am, but I know he likes to hold me, and I know I'm not too much for him. So I settle in, cuddling against his chest. "Aye, I met with them. Fools, the lot of them. When you left your father's lands, you took the only brain there with you."

I giggle.

He rubs my backside with one large hand. Months ago, I might have been mortified at such a show of affection, but now I just eat it up. "So, aye. We talked, and we talked, and he apologized quite a bit. Said there was a misunderstanding. That everything was blown out of sorts and there was no need to get the king involved. Oh, and I made sure to pass your letter on for your father."

"A misunderstanding, huh?" I shake my head. I shouldn't be surprised that my father is downplaying his threats to Agakor and his lands. They went on for a month or so, until the bleed of troops from my father's militia was so great that we had to actually start turning them away. True to his nature, my father was slow to pay, and that made more of his already questionable men leave. Meanwhile, Cragshold has been overflowing with soldiers, all being trained and given letters of recommendation when they head onward. Agakor says a trustworthy mercenary is worth every coin, and that he had to fight hard to get a good reputation, so he believes in supporting the men.

The men all admire him, too. Both orc and human, mercenary and knight, he's respected and friendly with all. He even knows the king of Adassia, the ruler called Mathior, who is king of three kingdoms—Adassia, Yshrem, and Cyclopae. I've never been so nervous as I was when Mathior visited for two days not long after our wedding, but it was a good visit. He bestowed a lordship title upon Agakor and his visit ensured that Agakor's claim on his lands is seen as a legitimate one. With our child on the way, my father has backed down and changed his story. My father is now saying he was simply concerned for my safety amongst all the "rough men" at Cragshold. That he never intended to pull me away from Agakor.

King Mathior just rolled his eyes at that, and I have to admit I laughed. My father is a weasel of the highest order, but at least the king is wise to his tricks so he can't pull them again. Ever since then, my father's men have been forbidden from trespassing on our lands. If my father should be found breaking this rule, Mathior's made it clear that Agakor has his support and not Father.

Which means things are quiet now, and we can focus on the baby. "What do you think my father will say when he reads the letter and finds out that we're having a child?"

Agakor tilts his head, gazing up at me. "Do you mean what I think he'll say publicly or what he'll say in private?"

I can't stop smiling. Maybe it's the pregnancy hormones, but gods, Agakor is the handsomest man to me. Rough featured, sure, and his broken tusk and equally broken nose will never impress the ladies at court, but he just takes my breath away. I stroke his cheek, unable to resist touching him. "Both?"

"I think publicly he will be thrilled for us. Privately I suspect he will have...colorful language."

Colorful indeed. Chuckling, I lean in and kiss Agakor on the mouth. His thick brows go up at my affectionate peck, and I can tell he's trying to decide if this is an invitation for a quick tumble before dinner or if I'm just happy. I decide it's both and give him another kiss. "I found a new book to read," I say in a light, carefree voice. "It's up in the solar. I thought we might read it together."

"Is that so?" He squeezes my arse.

I nod with a straight face. "But if you're too tired after riding all day—"

"Never too tired for a bit of, ahem, reading," Agakor states, and sets me on my feet. He's up out of the chair a moment later and slings his arm around my waist. "Come, my lady, and let us read for a few quiet hours before dinner."

Quiet hours of reading. It takes everything I have not to burst into laughter, because I know the moment we get into the solar, we're not touching the book. His head will be under my skirts and I'll be riding his face until he has me crying out with pleasure. Just the thought makes me squeeze my thighs together tightly. "Have I told you today that I love you?"

"At breakfast," he says, lifting my hand to kiss my knuckles. My big husband gives me a lascivious look. "You can tell me again when you're on my face."

Oh, I plan on it.

END

RUBY DIXON

Website: www.rubydixon.com
Facebook: www.facebook.com/RubyDixonBooks
Instagram: www.instagram.com/author.ruby.dixon/

Email: 1theclub1@gmail.com

Newsletter: www.rubydixon.com/wordpress/newsletter/
Reader Extras: www.rubydixon.com/wordpress/for-readers/

ABOUT RUBY

Ruby Dixon is an author of all things science fiction romance. She is a Sagittarius and a Reylo shipper, and loves farming sims (but not actual housework). She lives in the South with her husband and a couple of geriatric cats, and can't think of anything else to put in her biography. Truly, she is boring.

Made in the USA
Middletown, DE
27 September 2023

39488196R10132